CROSSING
THE
FARAK
RIVER

CROSSING
THE
FARAK
RIVER

MICHELLE AUNG THIN

annick press
toronto • berkeley

© 2020 Michelle Aung Thin (text)
Edited by Lyn White
Original Australian edition published in 2019 by Allen & Unwin
as part of the Through My Eyes series, under the title *Hasina*

Annick Press edition, 2020
Cover designed by Elizabeth Whitehead

Annick Press Ltd.

Library and Archives Canada Cataloguing in Publication

Title: Crossing the Farak River / Michelle Aung Thin.
Names: Aung Thin, Michelle, author.
Identifiers: Canadiana (print) 20190165545 | Canadiana (ebook) 20190168277 | ISBN 9781773213972 (hardcover) | ISBN 9781773213965 (softcover) | ISBN 9781773214009 (Kindle) | ISBN 9781773213996 (PDF) | ISBN 9781773213989 (HTML)
Classification: LCC PS8601.U54 C76 2020 | DDC jC813/.6—dc23

Published in the U.S.A. by Annick Press (U.S.) Ltd.
Distributed in Canada by University of Toronto Press.
Distributed in the U.S.A. by Publishers Group West.

Printed in Canada

annickpress.com
michelleaungthin.com

Lesson plan and e-book edition also available. Please visit annickpress.com for more details.

To the real Hasina,

who fled for her life to

the Myanmar/Bangladesh border

Myanmar is often still referred to by its former name, Burma. In this book, we use *Burma* to refer to the country prior to 1989. We use *Myanmar* to refer to the country after 1989. We use *Burmese* and *Myanmar* to refer to the peoples and language of Myanmar throughout this story.

BHUTAN

INDIA

BANGLADESH

KACHIN

SAGAING

CHINA

MYANMAR

CHIN

Arakan Mountains

Teknadaung*
(Hasina's Town)
Sittwe

RAKHINE

MANDALAY

SHAN

MAGWE

Irrawady River

Sittang River

KAYAH

LAOS

Bay of
Bengal

BAGO

YANGON

KAYIN

AYEYARWADY

MON

THAILAND

Andaman
Sea

TANINTHARYI

Gulf of
Thailand

N

0   200 km

*The town of Teknadaung is fictional

CHAPTER 1

Hasina has never heard anything like this strange sound coming from the sky. *Tocata tocata tocata*. It reminds her of her mother's old sewing machine. But instead of coming from another room, it is coming from above.

She stands in the middle of her family's vegetable garden, blinking her dark eyes against the November sun, looking for the source of that sound.

Tocata tocata tocata.

The sound has distracted her from a particularly juicy geometry problem. She was pulled to the window of her home schoolroom and then out the door and into the garden, the length of the right-angled triangle's hypotenuse left unsolved on the desk behind her.

Hasina isn't the only one drawn by the sound. Araf, her six-year-old brother, was the first outside, racing ahead of everyone. In fact, all the pupils at her aunt Rukiah's makeshift homeschool—Tara from the end of her road, Aman and Rosie from the next street over—are staring upward, while the ducks and geese that roam the garden rush about their legs. All of them have left the madrassa, the schoolroom with its shady thatch roof and woven bamboo walls that catch every breeze, to stand out here in the blistering sun. Even Aunt Rukiah has been lured outside.

"What is it, Hina?" Araf demands. "Is it *nagars*?"

Hasina smiles.

"No, Araf," scoffs their cousin Ghadiya as she limps toward them, the last one out of the madrassa. "It is not dragons. Dragons are not real."

"Are too," Araf mutters under his breath.

"Maybe it is a plane?" guesses wide-eyed Tara, fourteen years old like Hasina.

Hasina has heard the planes flying over her town of Teknadaung twice a week, from Sittwe, the capital. No plane has ever sounded like this.

"No," Ghadiya corrects Tara. Ghadiya is just thirteen, but her tone is superior. "Not a plane either."

Tocata tocata tocata. Like a needle going in and out of the cloth. A sewing machine in the sky. Except Hasina hasn't heard a sewing machine for nearly four years, not since the electricity was cut. Now her mother only sews by hand.

Hasina holds up her hand to shade her eyes against the late morning sun. That is when she sees them pop into view from the north. Eight bird-like creatures.

"There!" Hasina cries, pointing toward the eight dots. "I see them."

"Where?" shouts Araf. "*Where?*"

Hasina pulls him around in front of her and, bending low, rests her arm on her little brother's shoulder. She makes a square shape with both her hands, framing the eight birds. "Look along my arm."

Araf does, pointing his own fingers too. "I see them," he squeals. "I see the—the birds?"

"No, not birds either." Ghadiya's voice is wary now.

"What are they then?" Araf demands.

"Helicopters," Ghadiya says. It sounds like a warning.

Hasina shoots her cousin a surprised glance. Even though Ghadiya and Aunt Rukiah have lived with Hasina's family for years now, there are still things about Ghadiya that Hasina doesn't know. How does she recognize these dots as helicopters?

"Mama ..." Ghadiya's voice is a little wobbly, and Hasina sees that her face is pale. "Helicopters." She limps over to stand close by Aunt Rukiah, who puts an arm around her shoulders.

Hasina swings her gaze back to the eight dots, which are growing larger and larger. They are coming from over the Arakan Mountains that wall off Rakhine from the rest of Myanmar. They seem to be headed south toward the ocean, the big turquoise Bay of Bengal. Why would they head out over the water? Is there a cyclone coming? When Hasina was little, Cyclone Nargis flattened parts of Teknadaung. She remembers how the terrifying winds howled and the sky went dark. But this morning the sky is clear.

"*Toca toca toca,*" Araf shouts, imitating the sound.

"Time to go back inside, everyone." Aunt Rukiah's voice has an edge of fear to it.

But none of them move. Hasina doesn't think she *can* move. The birds are too mesmerizing. It's the sound they make, the rhythm of it. Their metallic gleam. Araf is right. They are like the *nagar*, the mythological dragons from her grandmother's stories.

A *nagar* comes whenever the world is about to change. Is the world about to change?

And just as this thought rises in Hasina's brain, the eight birds do another strange thing. Something Hasina has never seen birds do before, except one: the hawk.

The birds turn sharply and suddenly. They do this as one, keeping their formation the whole time. Sunlight flashes from their rotors as they change direction. They are not heading for the ocean anymore. Instead, they are heading directly for Teknadaung. In fact, it feels like they are coming straight for Eight Quarters, her neighborhood. For Third Mile Street. Her street.

And instead of flying high, they are dropping low. All eight birds move in perfect unison. All of them swoop like the hawk does when it takes a mouse.

Are they coming for *her*?

Closer and closer. Louder and louder. They don't sound like sewing machines anymore. They sound like a cyclone roaring onto land. The rhythmic *toca toca toca* becomes a *wop wop wop* so loud, so strong, that Hasina can feel it like she can feel her heart pounding inside her body.

Suddenly, Ghadiya screams, "Mama, they're green. They're Sit Tat."

Sit Tat. The name for the Myanmar Army. A word to send chills down the spine.

"Inside!" Aunt Rukiah roars, her voice jagged with panic. "Now!"

Tara, Aman, and Rosie turn and race for the madrassa. Aunt Rukiah sweeps Ghadiya under one arm and Araf under the other and drags them inside. The ducks and geese scatter.

But Hasina cannot move.

Hasina wants to run too. She wants to take shelter before the helicopters reach her house. But the sound pins her to the ground, the *wop wop wop* pressing down on her. She is paralyzed like the mouse when it feels the shadow of the hawk's wing.

"Hasina, run. *Run!*"

Closer and closer, lower and lower the helicopters come. Her head feels like it will burst with the din. Each sweep of the rotors surges in her chest. She clamps her hands over her ears. Around her, the air begins to swirl.

From inside the madrassa, Araf and Ghadiya are still calling to her. She sees their mouths opening and closing. *Run,* they are shouting, *run!*

But she can't.

And just as she is sure she will be crushed by those massive rotors, the image of an empty soccer net pops into her head. And into the net flies a soccer ball. Right into the back corner.

A perfect shot.

Hasina has made exactly such shots herself ... lined them up almost without looking. Imagined the ball into

5

the net so that all she had to do was be part of the movement, swing her foot to the ball and the ball into space.

Doors are rectangular, just like a soccer net.

And now she knows what she must do. Aim, shoot, and hope.

The first of the birds noses low over the garden as Hasina finds her legs again. Dust stings her eyes as she half-runs, half-scrambles, then launches herself toward the madrassa door, helicopters thundering overhead.

CHAPTER 2

"Hasina! What were you thinking?"

Hasina's breath comes in rough gasps. She is flat on her belly, arms spread in front of her. Every bit of her aches from smashing into the hard-packed dirt floor. Outside, the helicopters continue to clatter past.

"I said *run*." Aunt Rukiah's face is furious as she pulls her niece from the ground. "Why didn't you run?"

How can she explain the way the *wop wop wop* pinned her to the ground when she doesn't understand it herself? "I'm sorry, Aunty."

Aunt Rukiah's hands shake as she brushes the dirt from Hasina's *bazu* and *htamein*, cotton top and wrap-around skirt. "You don't mess with Sit Tat."

"I'm sorry."

"You don't know what they are capable of." Her aunt's harsh tone sounds closer to tearful now. "*I* know what they are capable of."

Hasina has heard Rukiah's stories before. They begin

with Sit Tat or Buddhist thugs or crooked police. They end abruptly with her aunt sobbing or ranting.

"I'm so sorry, *maja-fu*."

Aunt Rukiah pauses at the respectful term. The anger melts from her face as she tidies Hasina's long wavy hair back into a plait. "I am glad you are safe. Don't scare me like that again."

Aunt Rukiah and Ghadiya fled from the south of Rakhine province during the riots four years ago. Hasina doesn't really understand what the riots were about, just that the Buddhist Arakanese were angry with her people. All she knows is that when Aunt Rukiah, her *maja-fu* or father's sister, and Ghadiya came, it was without possessions. Almost everything they owned had been left behind. They came on foot, despite Ghadiya's limp, an injury from when she was born. They came without permits. Unlike any other of the groups who live in Rakhine—such as the Arakanese—Rohingya aren't allowed national registration cards and need special permits to travel. Worst of all, they came without Ghadiya's father, Rashid.

Hasina's cousin and aunt rarely speak about what they saw on that terrible journey. Or how they were separated from Uncle Rashid. But Hasina has her suspicions. She shares her bedroom with her cousin and has heard Ghadiya's nightmares, how her cousin calls out about men pounding at the door, and waves rising. Was it on that dangerous journey that Ghadiya learned about helicopters?

The madrassa is dark after the intensity of the light

outside, and Hasina still feels her eyes adjusting. Araf is at the window with the others, watching the helicopters pass. Ghadiya stands alone in the shadows of the room, her amber eyes wide in her round face as she listens to the sounds from the sky. Hasina can see the fingers of her right hand moving, as if she is counting the birds going past. Or maybe she is just willing them to go back over the mountains.

In her grandmother's stories, those rugged hills, covered with thick, emerald forest full of tigers and elephants, divide Rakhine from the rest of the country, so it feels like a land all of its own. Long ago, this was the kingdom of Arakan, an enchanted land according to her grandmother. Many of the people who live here feel it ought to be a kingdom once again, separate from Myanmar. Some of them, the Arakanese Army, are prepared to fight for this kingdom.

The Rohingya, Hasina's people, have also lived here for hundreds of years. That is the thing about this country, Hasina thinks; there are so many different types of people—Rohingya, Arakanese, Burmese, Mro, Shan, Kayan, to name just a few.

But these birds are not part of any enchanted tale.

"Heliwopters," shouts Araf. "*Wop wop wop wop wop.*"

Tara turns from the window. "Are they going away, *Saya?*" she asks, using the respectful term for teacher.

Aunt Rukiah's face is still pale. "I am not sure, Tara."

"*Saya,* will we be able to go home soon?" asks Rosie.

School was usually over after Dhurh, the second

prayers of the day just before lunch. *It must be well past Dhurh now*, Hasina thinks.

At least the *wop wop wop* is definitely fading.

"They're gone," Ghadiya announces to everyone, suddenly pushing away from her dark corner. She limps close to her mother and takes her by the hand. "And they won't be back, Mama."

Her cousin seems very sure about the helicopters leaving. Hasina watches the way her aunt's face softens with relief, how she nods to Ghadiya as if they are equals rather than mother and daughter. As if some secret knowledge is passing between them. If Ghadiya says the birds have gone, then as far as Aunt Rukiah is concerned, they have gone.

Hasina knows only too well that the violence four years ago touched every Rohingya family in Rakhine State. Cousins, uncles, grandchildren had to run away and were now scattered across the world. Many boarded leaky boats to Malaysia and Australia, and some have never been heard from again. Maybe they had died when those leaky boats capsized at sea. Others slipped overland across the border into Thailand, hoping they wouldn't be caught by army patrols or police. Others ended up in the internal displacement camps at Sittwe, Rakhine's capital. Others, like her aunt and cousin, traveled secretly to family in the north.

Even families like hers, here in the north where the Rohingya are in the majority, have been affected by the conflict her aunt calls the Arakanese War. First, the electricity, water, and gas were cut off. Then schools were closed or started charging such high fees to Muslims that even rich families could not afford to send their children any longer.

The violence has touched her family in other ways too. The changes in Hasina's own mother, Nurzamal, for example. Hasina remembers when she was little how her mother used to laugh, her large dark eyes dancing with light. She even recalls her mother stopping on their way to the family paddy field so that Hasina could practice dribbling her soccer ball on the open area by the Farak River. Now, Nurzamal is obsessed about doing things the *right* way. First, it was *Don't play soccer*. Then it was, *Hasina, be more modest. There are rules for Rohingya girls*. As if following rules more closely was the only way to keep safe. Even though all around them, it seemed the rules kept changing. And the more they changed, the less her mother seemed to want to hold Hasina or brush her hair or just laugh with her. Lately, Nurzamal has been talking about finding a husband for Hasina, someone to take care of her. To Hasina's relief, her grandmother Asmah refuses to even consider such a plan, although this makes Hasina sad too—it hurts to see her mother and her grandmother disagree.

Aunt Rukiah lets go of Ghadiya's hand. She turns to Tara, Aman, and Rosie. "School is over. It is safe to go home now." The three girls hastily gather up their books and head for the door. "Just make sure you finish your geometry before tomorrow," Aunt Rukiah calls after them.

Hasina follows her friends into the garden. "Bye." She waves.

"Goodbye," Tara calls back as she dashes through the gate.

Hasina squints up into the blue. The eight helicopters are dots on the opposite horizon now, well past the Farak River that divides Teknadaung in two. She has to listen hard to hear that *toca toca toca*. She cannot help but wonder where they are heading. She steps farther out into the garden for a better view when a sharp voice makes her jump.

"Hasina! Back inside at once." Nurzamal hurries from the kitchen, which is separate from the main house, and across the yard toward the madrassa. Her face is stern.

"Yes, Mama," Hasina replies.

She turns and follows her mother into the madrassa.

"Mama," Araf shouts, hurtling toward Nurzamal, who gathers him into her arms. Hasina's heart falls. How she would love to be gathered up in her mother's arms again, to breathe in her scent of kohl and clove and sandalwood.

"Did you hear the helicopters, Mama?" Araf asks, squirming in Nurzamal's arms as he waves his arms like a helicopter and squeals "*wop wop wop*."

"I did, my love. They came just before Dhurh."

The *azan*, call to prayer, for Dhurh used to float across the fields from the *mohzeem* but the police closed the town mosque a few months ago. The call to prayer now comes from the handsome wall clock Ibrahim, Hasina's father, brought home for his wife. It hangs just outside their bedroom. The clock's call would have come while the helicopters were overhead.

"Did you miss your prayers?" Nurzamal asks her son.

For a moment, Araf looks like he might cry. He adores his mother and fears disappointing her.

"We all missed Dhurh," Aunt Rukiah explains. "The helicopters were so loud. We can make it up later."

Nurzamal does not reply, and Hasina knows her mother can't help but feel that Aunt Rukiah and Ghadiya brought bad times with them. Seeing her mother and aunt side by side, Hasina is struck, as she often is, by how different they are—and not just in the way they think. Her mother's eyes are large and round, her nose straight, with a pronounced bridge; her skin is tea-colored, with roses in her cheeks, and her lush eyebrows meet in the middle. All of these mark her as a Rohingya. And Rohingya are not wanted in the land once known as Burma, and now known as Myanmar.

Her aunt on the other hand, who is also Rohingya, has a flat nose, and folded eyelids. Like Hasina's father, Ibrahim, and grandmother Asmah, Aunt Rukiah's skin is fair. In the bazaar no one would look at Aunt Rukiah twice without her *numal*, the headscarf that she wears in public as a polite Muslim woman. She could easily pass for Arakanese or even Myanmar.

Nurzamal gently prises Araf from her lap and stands up. "Hasina, your father's lunch is ready. You will take it to him at the bazaar. You are already late."

"But I still need to finish my geometry problem ..."

Hasina regrets her words almost as soon as they are out of her mouth. Nurzamal would prefer she went to a religious school rather than study math and history and geography in her aunt's madrassa. Yet Hasina suspects that her mother would have loved the chance to study herself; would still love the chance to read books and discuss ideas and think about the world.

Nurzamal's face tightens with anger. "We've already missed prayers. You want your father to miss lunch as well?"

"No, Mama." Hasina hadn't meant that.

As the eldest child in the family and without an older brother, Hasina has more responsibilities than other Muslim girls. Rohingya men usually do the shopping and take trips outside the home. If Hasina had an older brother, he would be taking his father's lunch to him.

"Can I go to the bazaar too, Mama?" Araf begs.

Araf loves the bazaar. He loves the family shop, where there are toy soldiers to play with. He loves his friends, the boys from neighboring stalls. But most of all, Araf loves the television set up at the entranceway. It is the only TV in all of Teknadaung, and sometimes it shows cartoons!

"Please, Mama, please please pleeeaaazzze!"

Whoa, Hasina thinks. For someone of just six, Araf is as deafening as any helicopter.

Nurzamal smiles; how Hasina loves to see her mother smile. Ever since Araf had fever a few years ago, Nurzamal has paid him extra attention. He is also a funny kid, dark like his mother, but with a knack for making people laugh. Both these things make him precious to Nurzamal. When she replies, her tone is unusually soft. "Of course. Someone needs to protect your sister. Hasina, you may take Araf. Now, go quickly to your bedroom and fetch your *numal*."

Hasina doesn't wear a *numal* indoors, but her mother insisted that she do so outside as soon as she turned thirteen. It is dignified, modest, and polite.

"You get your *numal* too, Ghadiya," Araf commands. "I will protect you as well."

Hasina sees a look pass between her mother and aunt. Although this house was Aunt Rukiah's home when she was a young girl, both she and Ghadiya are officially "foreigners" to the district—and illegal. Every trip out of the house risks arrest by police, heavy fines, bribes or worse. Ghadiya isn't allowed to go out much.

"No, Araf, Ghadiya is staying here," Aunt Rukiah says gently.

Ghadiya's face falls, and Hasina feels sorry for her cousin. Ghadiya might be bossy, she might like to show off, but having to stay home all the time must be pretty boring.

"Ghadiya, we can finish your geometry," Aunt Rukiah soothes. Ghadiya makes a face.

"Or you can come out and help me in the kitchen," Nurzamal offers. Despite everything, she is fond of her niece.

"Kitchen," Ghadiya says happily. Lunch is late and Nurzamal's kitchen is the best place to be when hungry.

CHAPTER 3

Hurrying to fetch her *numal*, Hasina dashes down the hall that runs alongside the madrassa and into the central part of the house. She loves her house made of thatch and wood and brick—a real patchwork, unique in Third Mile, where most houses are made of bamboo or wood. She skids past the wooden wall of Araf's room, then past the handsome clock outside her parents'' room.

Hasina breathes a sigh of contentment as she reaches her own beloved room. It is in the new part of the house, where the woven bamboo walls are perfect for the heat. There are two beds in the room, covered with identical striped bedspreads. Her grandmother, Dadi Asmah, jokes that the invisible line between Hasina's and Ghadiya's halves of the room is like the Farak River, dividing Teknadaung, for Hasina is tidy and her cousin very untidy.

Hasina pulls her headscarf from the chest of drawers. On her bedside table is a book in English, a few more in Burmese, and a notebook in which she likes to work out her thoughts. On the wall behind her bed is a poster of Sun Wen, the Chinese soccer star, in mid-air, the ball at the edge of her foot. Beside this is a poster of the mathematician Maryam Mirzakhani. An old, worn soccer ball sits in pride of place on a shelf.

Ghadiya's side of the room is a disaster zone. On the wall, three posters: one of the Burmese popstar Phyu Phyu Kyaw Thein, one of the pop group The Four, and the third a map of Malaysia where her father, Uncle Rashid, is. Her clothes, *htamein* and T-shirts, and *bazu* blouses she likes, litter the unmade bed. One object, however, is always neatly placed on the shelf—Ghadiya's tattered and faded orange cotton bag, a *lawl ait* from Shan State. It is the only thing that came with her from the south. Hasina has never seen her use it. As for what Ghadiya keeps inside, that is a secret. Hasina had a peek once, but the bag was empty.

Hasina quickly mixes a little water with *thanaka*, the sweet-smelling powder that everyone wears as sun protection in Myanmar, that she keeps in a jar on her dressing table. Sometimes Hasina paints *thanaka* onto her face in a leaf shape; other times, as a flower. But today, she hurriedly draws squarish patches on her cheeks with an old toothbrush—every female in Myanmar has a thousand uses for old toothbrushes and Hasina keeps several on her table. She checks herself in the mirror—a slender girl with long, wavy hair, dark eyes, skin tone halfway between that of her mother and aunt. Like her aunt, she can pass for Myanmar. Sometimes she wonders if her mother sends her to the bazaar to avoid the humiliating calls of *kalama* or black scum. The word makes Hasina burn with shame. She snatches up her orange and purple *numal*, and drapes it over her hair, tucking the ends around her neck, framing her face, before dashing from her room.

There is one small thing she wants to do before she heads out to the bazaar. Hasina's bare feet skid swiftly back along the hallway past her parents" room, and past the brick walls that mark the passage to her aunt Rukiah's room and her grandmother's beside it.

Dadi Asmah is as old as the house and the house is as old as Dadi Asmah. She has lived here all her life except for a few years at university in Sittwe. *This house,* Dadi Asmah likes to say, *is like this country. Lots of rooms, all different, but one house. Burma—lots of religions, lots of ethnic groups, lots of languages, all different, but still one country.*

Dadi Asmah looks a bit like her house—a mix of styles and races and dress. Her face is dominated by a hawk-like nose, but her eyes are gentle and she is inclined to smile rather than frown. She wears long blouses, like the Indian *kameez,* with Myanmar-style *htamein* or *longyi,* the wraparound skirt everyone wears. She prefers Myanmar-style sandals too. Her favorite head-gear is not a *numal,* but instead an ancient pith helmet she found in the bazaar long ago, left behind by some colonial gentleman. In the cool weather, Dadi Asmah loves a cricket cap.

Dadi Asmah's room has plastered walls, and pink English-style curtains pulled to screen out the harsh sunlight. Against a wall is a wooden bureau, where Dadi Asmah keeps her box of jewelry and her clothes. On top of the bureau are her photograph albums, a gramophone, and records. In a blue tin in the corner are Danish biscuits, brought out for very special occasions. Dadi Asmah loves biscuits and, truth be told, she is quite plump as a result.

Ghadiya loves playing with Asmah's jewelry. Araf loves the biscuit tin and gramophone records with their scratchy, tinny music. For Hasina, most delightful is the bookshelf. Books in Burmese, English, Urdu, and Bengali. Storybooks and atlases. History and biology. Hasina has loved to pore over these since she was a wee girl.

It is one of these same books that Asmah is reading, reclining on her bed.

"Dadi?" Hasina calls out softly, using the affectionate Rohingya term. "Dadi?"

Asmah drops the book onto her chest. Her large dark eyes peer over a pair of ancient reading glasses, held together with tape, now sliding down her nose. Asmah's black and gray streaked hair is piled up on top of her head and held with a clip. She smiles at Hasina. "My dear, please come in."

Hasina sits at the end of her grandmother's bed. This is her favorite spot in the whole world. She feels safe, more herself, when she is near her grandmother.

"Did you hear the birds, Dadi?"

"Yes, I heard them. But they did not sound like birds to me. Machines, perhaps."

"Ghadiya says they're called helicopters. Araf is calling them wop wops."

Asmah smiles and levers herself up into a sitting position, her back leaning against the wall.

"Wop wops is a good name."

"He thought they were *nagar*s." Princes of the ocean—dragons that could fly through the air and swim through earth as if it were water.

"I first saw helicopters when I was a young woman. There was a war in Bengal then. They terrified me."

"What do they mean, Dadi?"

Her grandmother quotes the old saying. "'*Kalaa ma naing Yakhine-meh*—if you want to learn how to keep the blacks in their place, go to Rakhine.' If I were a superstitious woman, I would call them *nagar*s too, for dragons breathe fire."

Hasina feels a spike of fear at her grandmother's words.

"But you say you do not believe in such superstitions, Dadi."

Her grandmother shakes her head "No. But those stories have power—that is why people believe them." She changes the subject. "Are you taking your father his lunch?"

Hasina smiles. Her grandmother knows that she often takes her father his lunch and shares it with him. But the question is part of a ritual between her and Dadi Asmah.

"Yes, Dadi."

"Then you will need this." Asmah reaches in under her *kameez* and unpins something from inside. She hands it to Hasina: a fifty-kyat note. "Buy yourself something nice."

Hasina hasn't the heart to tell her grandmother that these days you can't buy a thing for fifty kyats.

◈◈

Hasina adjusts her *numal* before shoving her feet into her sandals and crosses the yard to the kitchen.

The wooden kitchen is low and dark and sizzling with heat. It smells good. Wood burns in three stone braziers. Cast-iron pots bubble on top, one with fish curry, another with rice. On the third, a metal *deshi* cooking pot cools. The air is tangy with fish, coriander, ginger, and turmeric, the sweetness of rice, the sting of onion, and the perfume of wood smoke. An earthenware *chatty* pot, full of cool water for drinking, sits on a stand in one corner. On the square kitchen table lies a *suri*, a wide-bladed chopping knife. Oranges are piled in a bowl, and a bunch of bananas hangs from a cord slung from one side of the kitchen roof to the other. If you want to eat one, all you have to do is jump for it. Ghadiya and Araf are eating bananas now. Hasina hasn't eaten since early this morning and her belly gurgles.

Nurzamal hands Hasina her father's lunch, packed in tiffin carriers—three round metal containers stacked one on top of another, and held together with a handle. Hasina knows that inside will be *massor salon*, fish curry, made with onion, ginger, and garlic. Maybe a sweet-sour rice cake, rice with some dhal and lots of gravy, plus potato and greens and Kalarlay-brand special spice mix—her mother's secret ingredient. Hasina's mouth waters.

"Go straight to your father, Hasina," her mother commands. "Take the road, speak to no one."

"Are you ready, Araf?" Hasina asks her little brother.

"*Wop wop wop wop.*"

CHAPTER 4

The sun is high in the sky by the time Hasina and Araf turn out of their garden. Up and down Third Mile Street, families are getting ready for lunch. Delicious scents are in the air. Excitement too, thanks to the helicopters.

Hasina lives in Eight Quarters District, the Rohingya part of the town of Teknadaung. Eight Quarters sits between a bend in the Farak River and the paved "beach" highway that runs along the coast of Rakhine State and leads to Sittwe, the capital. Hasina was born here. Her father and aunt, her grandmother and great-grandmother, and so on and so on were born here too. She knows this place so well, she could walk blindfolded along this row of close-together houses and tell you exactly whose home she is standing in front of based on what she can smell cooking.

Today, for example, two doors down, there is the scent of *massor salon* with a dash of coconut. This is where Araf's friend Rehana lives. Sure enough, the little girl comes running as Araf passes.

"Araf, Araf, did you see the birds?" Rehana demands.

"They are called heliwopters," Araf informs her, knowledgeably.

Farther along the dirt road, a delicious smell of *hodu hak*, fried calabash, a long gourd, floats from Aziza Begum's kitchen. Every house on Third Mile Street is surrounded by gardens, where people grow their food. Vines are hung with *boothi*, a vegetable like zucchini. Pumpkin leaves, mounds of leafy cress, and pennywort grow in patches and rows. Ducks, chickens, and sometimes geese waddle and squawk. Aziza Begum's garden is the most sumptuously green and lush of them all. And her calabash are divine.

"*Aasso-lamu alaikum*." Hasina is quick to greet Aziza Begum politely in the Rohingya language, bowing her head. "Has Allah kept you well?"

"Aziza Begum," Araf calls, a little rudely, "did you see the birds? They are called heliwopters."

"*Wa alaikum aasso-lam*," Aziza Begum replies. "Yes, Allah has kept me well." Then, smiling, "Thank you, Araf, for your information."

The dhal at Hussain's house has a burnt smell. His lunch often gets scorched because he is too busy telling the children to stop playing and be quiet. In this close street, everyone mostly looks out for everyone else. Sometimes, Hasina feels there is a little too much of being watched over, and these houses, huddled together, can feel claustrophobic rather than protective.

At Tara's house, Monu Mush, her family's prized buffalo, is chained in the yard, stamping at the ground and eating sweet grass. Tara's mother, Sabikam Nahor, stops them with a friendly, "*Aasso-lamu alaikum.* How is your mother, Hasina?"

"Well, thank you."

Harvest is coming soon. Both Sabikam Nahor and Nurzamal are farmers' daughters, and the two families" paddy fields are side by side. At harvest time, they compete to see whose rice is best quality. Whose ducks are fattest. Who has the most ducklings. The biggest eggs.

Hasina loves watching her mother at work in the paddy field. Nurzamal knows how to read the soil, when to drain the field, when to introduce the ducks. Since she was a little girl, Hasina remembers watching the ducklings grow as the rice got taller and greener until finally it was ready to harvest. Every year, there is hard work, special foods and drinks, stories told by the older women, jokes and games. And her mother at the center of it all. Harvest is the happiest of times. Why, then, does this year bring her feelings of foreboding?

"Sabikam Nahor," Araf asks shyly, "did you see the metal birds?"

"See them! I had to come out and soothe Monu Mush." Sabikam Nahor loves Monu Mush almost as much as she loves Tara and her other children. "You were frightened, weren't you, Monu? Poor thing."

"Heeeyoouuuuu," bellows Monu Mush, tossing his handsome head.

"Phoo," exclaims Araf, as he ducks behind Hasina. "Monu Mush has very big horns."

"Time to go!" Hasina takes her brother's hand in hers.

At the end of Third Mile Street, Hasina begins to shake off some of the morning's drama. She can feel a cool breeze on her face as they turn toward the Farak River. The air is scented with coconut palm and river water and new growth.

Hasina and Araf stop at the standpipe at the top of Third Mile Street.

Every morning after Fagr, first prayers at 5:40 a.m., Hasina and Ghadiya trudge here, half-asleep, to fill up big buckets with water for the family and carry them back balanced on their heads. That water has to last them all day long. Water carrying is a job Rohingya girls do. It is hard work; very hard work. But mostly the two cousins enjoy being out together in the early morning. Besides, Hasina reminds herself, it is great training to keep her fit for soccer—if she ever gets to play again! In the evenings they return for washing and teeth-brushing, girls at one time, boys at another.

It was on one of those mornings that Ghadiya hinted at what she had seen on the dangerous journey north.

She and Hasina had been playing hide-and-seek in the long grass beside the road when Ghadiya let out a sharp scream. She seemed transfixed by an old rag lying draped over clumps of grass, and at first Hasina thought her cousin had seen a snake crawl under it.

Hasina bent over to lift it up carefully. *It's just a piece of cloth, see? It's only an old* longyi *someone has thrown away.*

No! Ghadiya screamed and turned away.

But there's nothing here, Hasina soothed. *Have a look.*

Ghadiya had not wanted to have a look. Instead, she limped ahead as fast as she could, stopping only when she was at the pump. She washed her hands again and again, scrubbing them until they were red. Only then did she offer an explanation in a flat voice.

There was a girl I met on the way here. Her name was Rivka. She died. They covered her with a longyi *and left her in the field.*

She has never spoken about it again.

Hasina puts her father's tiffin down on a large flat rock. She is hungry and thirsty, and there is still a long way to walk.

"Are you ready for a drink, Araf?"

"Yes! I am *very* thirsty."

Hasina leans on the long pump handle with both hands and her whole weight. Slowly, the handle shifts. Then, she hauls the handle hard upward. Down then up, down then up, she pumps harder and harder until her arms burn and her breath comes in gasps. It takes several minutes of pumping before the pressure builds up and the water begins to rise.

"Let me pump," Araf pleads. "I am very strong."

"Okay, get ready…"

She pumps for a few more strokes. Only when it

is easy and the pump is loose does she let Araf place his tiny hands at the bottom of the handle.

"One, two, three, four ..." Araf counts. Magically, water streams from the nozzle.

Araf squeals his delight and immediately lets go to cup his hands beneath the gush. Hasina is ready for him, holding tightly to the handle so it doesn't fly upward. The last thing she wants to do is break the pump. She knows how very lucky they are to have a standpipe on Third Mile Street. Ever since the water supplies were cut at Eight Quarters, four years ago, girls from other parts of Teknadaung have had to walk half an hour one way and then another half-hour back from the river or creek nearest to their home.

Hasina watches as Araf drinks deeply, then braces herself.

"It's raining," Araf cries, splashing water all over Hasina.

Hasina laughs. "It's pouring," she shouts, splashing him back before bending her own head to the pipe to drink. It is an old rhyme Asmah taught them.

The water is cool and tastes of earth. It feels cool on her skin too, especially with the breeze from the river. *Ah, that is better.* She stands up and eases her shoulders before drinking in the landscape.

Long, long ago, Asmah would begin another of her stories, *before your great-grandmother and even your great-great-great-great-grandmother were born on this very spot, people from all around the Bay of Bengal came to Arakan to trade and see its wonders. They didn't need roads; the rivers, streams and brooks were the roads, and you could paddle up and down between the villages or sail from settlement to settlement along the bay.*

Hasina loves the lush heart of Rakhine best. Ahead of her, the jade-green hills slope down from the mountains. Water from the frequent rains that fall from April to November drains along these slopes and runs into rivers, tracing Rakhine over and over again with streams and *chaungs*, smaller waterways. From one season to the next, the whole countryside changes. Hasina loves how one month, you might live in a field; the next, on an island. How you might see a bridge swinging over air and know that the air would become a river during the rains. All those rivers and streams were now full. In November, one could go anywhere by boat. As for fishing, well, as Dadi Asmah says, *Just dip your fishhook into the water to bring up something tasty for your dinner.*

It is the Farak River that they must cross now to get to the bazaar where her father waits for his lunch. All the talk of helicopters with their neighbors has delayed them. Her father will be hungry. She herself is ravenous.

Three paths open out before her. To the left, a narrow, raised, sandy footpath leads to the Lower Forest, a stand of palms and teak trees. This shady forest, only a few hundred meters away, is where Hasina and Ghadiya gather wood for cooking. The bazaar, on the other hand, is at the center of Teknadaung, which lies across the river. There are two ways to get there. The long way and the short way.

The long way is south, along the river toward the

Rohingya paddy fields, and the paved road leading to the metal bridge over the Farak. This is also the way to the wide piece of open ground where Hasina used to play soccer. With a pang she realizes it has been over a year since she last ran up and down, dribbling the ball past her friends. None of her girlfriends are allowed to play soccer anymore. Hasina misses those games, standing with her back to the river and looking out across the paddy fields, sometimes even seeing her mother at work.

But there is a shorter way to the center of Teknadaung. The bazaar is actually directly ahead, in a straight line from the standpipe. If you cross the river right here, you could be there in fifteen minutes. Problem is the Farak River. It rises, it falls. There are dangerous currents.

The short way means crossing the Children's Bridge, a floating bridge made of three pontoons tied together with big ropes that loop around wooden posts rammed low into both riverbanks. The bridge rises when the rivers and creeks fill up at the end of the monsoon. If you didn't know where it was, you wouldn't know it was there. But every kid in Eight Mile knows the bridge. Dadi Asmah remembers the same bridge from when she was a child. Just like in her day, there is only a rope handrail.

The Children's Bridge is fun; the pontoons tilt crazily under your weight. That tilting makes it dangerous for adults. Anyone weighing more than a child risks being dumped into the deep, fast water. Children too have been swept away. Nurzamal has forbidden Hasina and Araf from using the bridge under any circumstances. At fourteen, Hasina is almost too big for the bridge. As for Ghadiya, she hates the Children's Bridge. Her limp makes the pontoons feel too unstable and the rushing water terrifies her.

But sometimes, Hasina tells herself, *you need to take a risk, break the rules a little.*

"Araf, can you keep a secret?"

"I am very good at keeping secrets."

"We are going to cross the Children's Bridge. But you have to promise not to tell Mama. Or she will be angry."

"Promise." Then, as if to prove it, Araf runs ahead of Hasina, scampering down the steep bank to the pontoons.

"Araf!" Hasina calls. "Wait!" She scrambles down the riverbank after him.

Araf may be too short for the hand rope, but he is agile. He holds on to a stake as he lowers himself onto the first pontoon, which barely shifts beneath his weight. He is across it in a flash.

"Whoa, Araf!" Hasina shouts. "Be careful!"

"Be quick." He grins back, jumping onto the next pontoon and the one after that. In a moment, he is at the top of the other bank.

Hasina casts a glance upstream as she crosses the bridge. Beneath the pontoons, she can feel the current of the river. The banks rise high, so high she cannot see above them. What she can see, looming over her from the north, is the High Forest, a dark and sinister tangle of palms and teak and banyan trees on top of rocky hills that rise above the Arakanese paddy fields on one side and end in cliffs on the other. Ogres and tigers lurk in these knotted woods.

If you are naughty, Nurzamal and every other parent in Teknadaung say, *I will take you to the High Forest and leave you there.*

Hasina has never been in the High Forest. Even though it is broad daylight, and she is too old for tales of ogres, looking up into those trees still makes her shudder. She forces herself to turn away and follows Araf up the riverbank and into town.

CHAPTER 5

On the other side of the river, Teknadaung changes. The Farak divides Muslim on one side from Buddhist on the other.

It wasn't always that way, Dadi Asmah has told Hasina. *Once, Muslim and Buddhist, Rohingya and Arakanese lived side by side with all the others too. That's why the old mosque is just a few blocks from the bazaar.*

Hasina still misses the *azan* floating across the fields, marking the moments that made up your day.

Hasina hurries Araf up the hill through the Arakanese paddy fields and toward the bazaar. As they rush up the main street, she is careful not to catch the eyes of the officers in blue and gray as they pass the police station. She keeps her face to the ground as they pass the old Portuguese fort walls, where Arakanese men sit and spit betel juice at the ground. She glances to see if the foreigners have opened the International Aid office. When she and Araf come to the Basic Education

School, the government school where she used to learn, she cannot help but stop.

She scans the yard, looking for a familiar face. A group of boys hit a woven rattan ball up into the air with their knees, feet or elbows. They twist and turn, doing whatever they have to do to keep the *chinlone* ball off the ground. They would make great soccer players, Hasina thinks. On a shaded bench, two girls sit with an open textbook, talking over some problem. Hasina wonders if it is a math book. In another part of the yard, four girls run after a soccer ball, their plaits flying behind them. But she doesn't see anyone she knows.

Araf pulls at her arm. "Let's go."

Still, she lingers.

It has been four years since Hasina was forced to leave government school. How she wishes she could wear one of those green and white school uniforms again. Green is the color for learning, and teachers in Myanmar and all students wear crisp white shirts with a green *longyi*.

Hasina sighs. She is lucky, she knows that. When she was little, Dadi Asmah insisted she go to school and paid for it as long as possible too. She has Aunt Rukiah, a real teacher. But still. To have conversations about what is in the textbook. To *have* a textbook. To fly around the paved yard like those girls, chasing a soccer ball. These girls have nice faces. They might have been her friends, even though she is a Rohingya.

Suddenly, Hasina feels very old. Fourteen *is* old. Fourteen is thinking about getting married. Fourteen is thinking about a husband. And children.

"Come on!" Araf tugs at her hand.

Just then, the girl with the longest plait swipes the soccer ball too hard and it flies out the gate. Instinctively Hasina lunges, catching it with her right foot before flicking it back in a perfect arc. The girl scoops it up and gives her a thumbs up, then drops the ball and plays on as if nothing has happened.

"Come on, Hasina! TV!"

"Coming." She grins at Araf.

Hasina and Araf thread their way through the clutch of bicycles and motorbikes that crowd the front of the bazaar. They dodge the country women, their vegetables and fish laid out for sale on old *longyi*s at the entrance.

The bazaar is at the top of a hill in a direct line from the riverside docks. Her father once told her that the British built the bazaar in exactly this spot so that they could roll barrels of toddy rum and rice down the hill and straight into the hull of the ships that used to sail up the river.

Old as the bazaar is, there are older things in Teknadaung. The golden stupa, for example, that gleams high up against the dark green of the forest and marks an age-old Buddhist shrine. Or the wall of blue painted stones, remains of a forgotten palace. Near the river, a Christian cross marks the ruins of a Portuguese church. Dadi Asmah used to point these things out to Hasina when she was little, saying that in these buildings you could read the whole history of not just Rakhine, but of Burma too.

Suddenly Araf drops her hand. "Catch me!" he

shouts, hurtling off as fast as his six-year-old legs allow, ducking past bicycles, leaping over an elderly woman selling mustard greens.

Hasina laughs. Araf is annoying, Araf is noisy, but he is also predictable. She knows he is heading straight for the television at the front of the bazaar, where the Arakanese stalls are. Nurzamal would have stopped him with tales of small boys being kidnapped to be sold as slaves to highway teashops, where the big trucks pass. Hasina isn't sure if these stories are true or just for scaring children. Besides, if there is one place where she feels most comfortable in all of Teknadaung, it is the bazaar.

People still mix here as they did in the old days. Something about entering that building makes her forget what is going on outside. This is where people come for news as well as shopping. Hasina loves the smells— spices, delicious things frying, fabrics and *thanaka*, perfumes from places like Arabia and America. She loves threading her way through the narrow little laneways to her family stall, which is at the other side of the building in the Rohingya section.

But when Hasina arrives at the front of the bazaar, it is to find a knot of people staring up at the TV. Araf is standing by himself, off to one side, also watching.

It seems like all the Arakanese men and women of the bazaar are here. Hasina can't see any of the Rohingya stallholders who normally stop to watch. A news program is on the screen, the announcer speaking in Myanmar. Thanks to Aunt Rukiah's lessons and Dadi

Asmah's bookshelves, Hasina knows fluent Burmese. The announcer's voice is quick and excited, and she is talking about Muslims: specifically, Chittagonian Bengali Muslims.

This is the name the government insists on using instead of *Rohingya*, which is not allowed. Using *Rohingya* is to admit that Hasina's people are at home in Myanmar, and are one of the original groups, or what the government calls *taing-yin-thar*. *Bengali* implies they are foreigners, from Bangladesh—strangers who do not belong here. Those words, *Chittagonian Bengali* Muslims, always make Hasina feel uneasy. She knows that she is Rohingya. It hurts her to think of herself as nameless in the same way it hurts that she can't go to school.

But then the announcer uses a word that makes Hasina's blood run cold. *Terrorist. Muslim terrorist.* There are other words that the announcer shortens to ARSA. This is new to Hasina, but instantly she knows it must be even worse than being called Bengali. *Terrorist* means someone who is dangerous rather than simply unwanted.

Again and again the announcer repeats two words. Always together. *Terrorist and Muslim. Muslim and terrorist. Muslim terrorist.*

Muslim, like her and Araf.

Does that mean that everyone here, watching the TV, will think they are also terrorists?

CHAPTER 6

Hasina feels like she has swallowed a stone. Suddenly, her *numal* doesn't feel dignified or modest or even polite. Instead, it feels like something that marks her out, that draws attention to her. *Muslim.*

Hasina watches as flames from a burning building flicker across the television screen, followed by a picture of soldiers running, their guns pointed. Then there is a picture of women sitting on the ground crying. Then police in blue and gray uniforms walk along a street just like Third Mile Street. The voice in Burmese goes on and on. The announcer sounds serious and angry. She talks about Sit Tat, the Myanmar Army. She talks about terrorists. She uses the term *ARSA* again and again.

But even though the announcer is talking about people and groups Hasina's never met, or even heard of, she feels as if the announcer is speaking directly to *her*. As if all this is *Hasina's* fault. As if Hasina herself is a terrorist.

Lucky none of the men have noticed her. They are

all watching the screen, arms crossed tight against their bodies. She can see their fear rising, their anger too. The women are putting hands on hips. Hasina feels the stone in her stomach getting bigger and bigger. She reaches for her brother's hand, holds it tight. If they're quiet and quick, maybe they can retrace their steps and circle the building. They could enter the bazaar from another door, the door nearer the Rohingya stalls. They must avoid these angry people who are now scared of Muslims who are also terrorists. She's gently pulling Araf away when the image on the TV screen changes.

Suddenly, there are helicopters just like the ones they saw this morning. The men and women beneath the screen murmur and gasp their recognition. Araf pulls his hand from hers and points a stubby finger at the screen and in loud, piercing Rohingya language, cries, "Look, Hasina! Look!"

All the Arakanese stallholders turn to face Hasina and Araf.

A dozen angry men and women who have just been hearing all about Muslim terrorists now turn to find a Muslim—a Rohingya Muslim—in front of them.

Hasina feels their eyes burning into her as they take in her *numal*. The stone in her stomach gets heavier. Will she have to run from these people? Isn't that what Ghadiya said happened down south—that angry Buddhists started to attack her people? If she has to run, where is there to go? How will she take Araf with her? The stone in her stomach will slow them both down.

And then Araf does it again.

"Heli*wop*ter," he calls out, as loud as anything.

"Heli*wop*ters?" a man beneath the TV says out loud.

"*Wop wop wop*," Araf replies.

Hasina holds her breath. The whole of the bazaar seems to hold its breath. They are waiting to see what the Arakanese man will do, deciding if they're going to be angry or not.

The man's round Arakanese face is kind; his eyes twinkle as if to ask, *What does this* wop wop wop *mean*? He looks the same age as her father. Maybe he has children himself. Maybe he has a little boy like Araf. He looks puzzled, not angry. But puzzled can so quickly become angry.

Hasina tightens her grip on Araf's hand. If they need to run, which way? Right or left? Are they small enough to wriggle through the tiny passageway between the stalls and evade capture?

Then the man starts to laugh. "*Wop, wop, wop, wop?*" He smiles and nods at Araf.

"*Wop wop wop*," Araf says back.

Then the Arakanese man reaches up and turns the dial to another TV channel. Bulldozers run across a farmer's land. A Burmese voice drones on about rice and the harvest, a few weeks away. The knot of adults relaxes. Some of them drift away. An Arakanese woman turns and smiles kindly at Hasina.

Hasina lets out a long breath of relief before taking Araf's hand to drag him away.

"But Hina, why can't I watch cartoons?" he whines.

She squeezes his hand tighter and growls, "Baba is

hungry." Instantly she thinks how she sounds just like her mother. Stern. Forbidding. She sighs. "You can watch cartoons later. I will take you."

"Promise?"

"Promise."

CHAPTER 7

Hasina steers Araf toward the back of the bazaar, where the Rohingya stalls are. All around her now are the familiar faces. Here is the scent of cumin and cardamom. Voices all around them speak in Rohingya. The men wear white *tufih*, caps, and the women, *numal*s.

"Bashy!" Araf sudddenly shouts.

Up ahead is the Brothers & Sons Puppet Stall. Fantastic creatures with papier-mâché faces wearing gorgeous costumes of red, blue, orange and pink hang from strings across a dais, sometimes an impromptu stage. Amir, one of the brothers, sits on this platform, in front of a roller door, sipping his tea while making a warrior king dance. Out front two boys, one small, one big, hunker over a basket that seems to move on its own. *Is it a new kind of puppet*, Hasina wonders, *one without strings?*

The small boy looks up. "Araf!" Bashir squeals, several decibels more piercing than even Araf.

"We saw heli*wop*ters!" Araf sprints toward his friend.

"We have *kittens!*" Bashir raises both arms in the air over the wobbling basket.

So that is what is in the basket! Hasina laughs out loud as boys and kittens tumble together in a blur of fur and feet, claws and fingers.

Now the bigger boy, Isak, looks up. He catches Hasina's eye and grins.

And just like that Hasina's heart beats faster. This time, not with fear. At least, not fear of helicopters or angry stallholders.

Ever since she was a little girl, Isak has been part of her life. When they were allowed to go to the government Basic Education School, his desk was alongside hers. When the school started to charge high fees to Rohingya pupils because they weren't *taing-yin-thar*, he stayed while most others left. When school fees rose again and again and again until no Rohingya could afford them, he came to Hasina's father Ibrahim's stall for lessons. He was the gangly kid she could outrun and outshoot on the soccer field. Now that gangly kid is tall and broad. Same brown eyes, same dark eyebrows, same crinkly grin, same tight curls beneath his *tufih*. But one morning, when she saw him standing at the Brothers & Sons Puppet Stall, she realized that he was also beautiful.

"*Aasso-lamu alaikum.*" She greets Amir in the Rohingya language, bowing her head, then turns to Isak. "*Aasso-lamu alaikum.*" Hasina is thankful that her *numal* helps hide the blush she feels spreading across her cheeks.

"*Wa alaikum aasso-lam*," Isak replies, then, "*Ken ah so?* How are you, Hasina?"

Isak and Bashir are two of the three sons from the Brothers & Sons Puppet Stall. Their father, Amir, and their uncle, Sultan, opened the stall as young men. When their children came along, they added *Sons* to the name. The third son is Jamaal, Sultan's son.

"Look at this kitten, Hasina."

Isak gestures to a tabby with distinctive blue eyes and bends to gently pick her up, cradling the tiny creature in his strong, slender hands. He brings the kitten's face close to his.

"She is too clever to get into that ruckus." He turns to Hasina and smiles again. "Clever like you."

Hasina's belly does a little flip. *He thinks I'm clever!* It is all she can do not to break into a huge smile. Luckily, Isak is too busy meowing at the kitten to notice Hasina is blushing again. The little cat mews back, showing tiny, sharp teeth. Isak laughs and gently lets the kitten loose onto the ground, where she immediately rubs herself against Hasina's legs.

"She likes you."

"What is her name?"

"Daamini."

It means lightning. And Daamini quickly shows why the name suits her. She waves her tail and hunkers down into a hunting position. Slowly, carefully, she advances one paw, then another, before pouncing on a big beetle. The beetle is fast but the kitten faster. She proudly turns to Isak and drops the beetle at his feet.

"See that? It is exactly how you used to score a goal when we played soccer." Isak laughs, then his tone turns serious. "You saw the helicopters?"

Hasina nods. "My aunt says they are Sit Tat." She keeps her voice low.

"Jamaal thinks so too." Isak lowers his voice farther. "He says there have been attacks on the border police. That police have been killed."

The border police are almost as scary as the Sit Tat. They take Muslim men to the station and beat them up. They charge Muslim businesses extra taxes or protection money. It was hard to know when—or *if*—you could trust them. But attacks? *Terrorist attacks*, the TV reporter said.

Hasina felt the stone in her belly again.

Isak continued. "Jamaal says it is ARSA."

ARSA. The name she'd heard on the broadcast. "What is ARSA?"

"Arakan Rohingya Salvation Army. Jamaal says they are fighting for the Rohingya."

Hasina has heard her father and aunt talking about another army—the Arakan Army—who were fighting to make Rakhine a country of its own. But this ARSA, a Rohingya army—this is new to her.

Isak leans in a little closer. "Jamaal says that they are looking for men to join them. To become soldiers."

His eyes take on a distant look. Hasina knows that look well, although she does not understand it. Sit Tat are feared, yet all the boys she knew at school dreamed of becoming a soldier and all the girls dreamed of marrying soldiers.

Is Isak thinking of joining ARSA? The stone in her belly grows heavier.

A yowl from one of the kittens is followed by a yelp from Araf. Isak resumes his gentle self. "Are you okay, Araf?"

"The kitten won't let me pull her tail."

Isak frowns gently at Araf. "Always better to be kind, Araf."

"Time to get lunch to Baba. Come, Araf." Hasina turns to Isak. "Goodbye."

"Allah keep you safe," Isak returns.

Safe. That is what she wants for Isak too. All the way to her father's stall, she thinks about ARSA and the news that they are recruiting young men. Boys, really. Boys like Isak.

Boys who would have no chance against Sit Tat.

CHAPTER 8

Hasina's family shop is at the back of the Rohingya section of the bazaar, in a wide corner spot. It was Hasina's grandfather who opened it, but it is her father who has made a success of the stall. Today, he sits in front of it reading a newspaper.

Hasina feels proud of the shelves lined with expensive plastic-wrapped things. There are individual packets of shampoo, colored bright pink and yellow and orange. Danish biscuits, tins of sweetened condensed milk, or *dut*, batteries and matches and tiny scissors and tweezers and a bucket of plastic toy soldiers—Araf's favorites. There are sachets of Tea Mix—very strong tea powder with the milk and sugar already mixed in, just add water—as well as little green packets of instant coffee and coffee creamer. These things are the wealth of her family and just running her eyes along these rows gives Hasina a warm, safe feeling. But what she loves best about the bazaar is spending time with her father. She enjoys watching how his face changes expression as he reads his newspaper or the way he puts his fingers to his head before he gives an answer or voices an opinion.

"Baba," Araf calls out. Pulling his hand from Hasina's, he runs to their father, who looks up with a smile.

Like his sister, Aunt Rukiah, Ibrahim's skin is fair and his eyes are long and tucked in a fold of skin. He dresses like an Arakanese or Myanmar businessman, in a *longyi* but with a crisply ironed button-up shirt. When it is chilly, he adds a sports coat.

Ibrahim is a man of learning. Unlike many Rohingya, he has had formal schooling to the tenth standard. His own parents—Hasina's grandparents—were both university graduates. Among the Rohingya, it is only the old people who have been to university. When a neighbor, a fellow stallholder, or someone from the mosque needs help with a form or a notice, it is to Ibrahim they turn. Men come to the stall not just to buy, but also to ask. Ibrahim helps not only the Rohingya, but also the Arakanese who live and work nearby.

What he asks of himself, he also asks of Hasina. On quiet days, he sets figures in front of her to add or subtract, multiply or divide. Or the newspaper so she can practice reading Myanmar script. He has done this since she was a little girl.

Each time she adds up a column of figures, reads the news aloud, walks through Teknadaung with Araf, she thinks, *I am seeing into the world of men.* The thought intrigues her, and she dares to wonder why it is that men go to the mosque while women pray at home. Why men do the shopping while women do not.

The back of the stall is partitioned off by a curtain. In this small space is a plastic table and chairs where Ibrahim sits to do the accounts. Above these is another handsome wall clock that calls out the times for prayer, plugged into an electric outlet. In this little alcove, Ibrahim keeps the book of accounts, a strongbox and a blanket. Hasina sets out the blanket on the floor of the stall for lunch and places the tiffin boxes in the center.

"So, my children." Ibrahim smiles, lowering himself on the blanket. "What is the news today?"

"Baba, we saw heliwopters."

"Heliwopters? What might those be?"

"Great big metal birds like *nagar*s!" Araf shouts. "They flew right over our house, Baba. And Hasina got trapped outside. I had to rescue her!"

Hasina's mouth falls open. "How did you rescue me?"

"I shouted *run*," Araf says triumphantly. Then his face falls. "But they came before Dhurh and we missed prayers."

"We will make it up at Asr." Ibrahim turns to his daughter. "And you, Hasina, what do you make of these helicopters?"

Hasina shivers at the memory of those terrifying birds. How they frightened her all over again when she saw them on TV.

"I think I would be glad not to see them again."

A look passes between father and daughter as if to

say, *We will talk about this later*. Ibrahim changes the subject. "Now, what is this?"

"This is lunch. And I am hungry," answers Araf.

Ibrahim smiles and turns to unstack the three metal containers. "What is in here?" he asks Araf, even though lunch is always the same. "Is it ... chicken curry?"

Araf erupts into snorts of laughter. Chicken is for special occasions. Like getting married, when an entire, egg-laying chicken is cooked for the bridegroom.

"Well then, is it a soft drink? Cola? Lemonade?"

Araf laughs even harder, and Hasina can't help but grin. Who has money for drinks in a tin?

"Let's see then." Ibrahim flips the metal lid from the first tiffin tin, releasing the aroma of garlic, ginger and fish. "Ah, your mother's *massor salon*."

"Yum," says Araf. Hasina's tummy rumbles so loudly she has to put her hands over her belly to suppress the sound.

Ibrahim lifts the next lid.

"Vegetables!" Araf smacks his lips. Tasty *hori hak*, pumpkin leaf, from the garden, cooked with smashed garlic.

"Well, then this must be ... rice?" Ibrahim flips the last lid, and the floral fragrance of rice fills Hasina's nostrils. She should wait for her father and brother to eat first, but cannot help the saliva from rising in her mouth.

Ibrahim places a tiffin tin lid in front of Araf and another in front of Hasina. He takes the flat *shamish*, spoon, from inside the rice tin and scoops rice, vegetables and fish curry onto his own lid. Then, using the fingers of his right hand, he wets the rice with the vegetables and fish gravy before shaping it into a pyramid with his fingers and holding the morsel to his mouth.

"*Bismillah karo hamam rahin.* In the name of Allah, gracious and merciful." Then he pops the lot into his mouth. "Mmmhmm." He savors the salty, slurpy, fishy flavor. "Eat," he says.

Hasina waits for Araf to scoop himself a tiny mound, then it is her turn to use the *shamish* to scoop up rice, fish curry and vegetables onto her lid. The rice is warm and each grain firm to the touch as she pushes curry, green leaves and rice into a pyramid, rich and spicy and slurpy and delicious. She is just about to slide the whole morsel into her mouth when a familiar gruff voice calls out behind her.

"*Mingalar bar.*"

Hasina jumps, startled. A shadow looms over the three of them. She looks up into a wide, bloated face, a false smile showing big yellow teeth.

It is U Ko Yin, the teashop owner.

CHAPTER 9

Hasina drops her food back onto the lid. She turns to U Ko Yin and drops her head and joined hands toward him, bowing in a *shi-kho*, Myanmar-style, a polite way to greet older people. Then she pulls away from lunch and tucks herself behind the small curtain across the alcove. If U Ko Yin notices her, he does not say anything. Instead, he greets Araf and Ibrahim.

"Look at you, Araf—such a big boy. Time for you to go to work! Come and work in my teashop. We could use a boy like you."

Ibrahim compresses his lips into a tight line but keeps his voice polite. "Araf is still a little boy. Too young for work."

"Ah," scoffs U Ko Yin, "it is never too soon to learn."

U Ko Yin's teashop, a few doors down, is called Lucky 7. Most teashops are busy selling good, cheap food and pots of tea. But Lucky 7 is never busy. Hasina has often heard her father say that nobody likes U Ko Yin's teashop because he is always watching whether customers use too much sugar or don't order enough. He often comes over to Hasina's father's stall to moan about his lack of customers.

"Helicopters, *la*," he says to Ibrahim, "so bad for business. Oh dear, is that your lunch? I wondered what I smelled."

That is the other thing about U Ko Yin—he has a knack of arriving at lunchtime, even though Buddhists generally eat before noon and Muslims eat much later.

"Would you like to join us?" Ibrahim asks politely.

"Well ... perhaps a mouthful, just this once ..."

U Ko Yin heaves his *longyi*-clad bottom onto the very spot on the floor that Hasina has just vacated. His knees creak beneath his weight. He dips his thick fingers directly into the tiffin tins, pinching out a large mouthful of rice, curry and vegetables, which he pushes into his mouth.

"Of course, my preference is for the Pathein rice. Bigger grains, stickier." He licks his fingers as he talks. "This is good too. Just not what I am used to."

From behind her curtain, Hasina wishes she had brought her little lid of lunch with her. She hears the grunt as U Ko Yin reaches for more food, then another grunt as he leans back again. It doesn't sound like he is going anywhere. He starts to complain about business.

"Ever since that fighting in the south, four years now, *la*. Nobody goes out, nobody eats noodles, nobody drinks tea. And now, these army helicopters ..."

So those *were* army helicopters, just as Ghadiya said.

"Of course," U Ko Yin continues, "things would be better if I had a good location, like this one. You are lucky in business, *la*."

U Ko Yin exhales heavily.

"But Sit Tat, the AA and now this ARSA—Muslim terrorists, acting against their own people. Here I am, a businessman, what do I care for politics? But all this is bad for business. You mark my words, soldiers will come. They will come here, to Teknadaung."

Is it true? Would soldiers come? Could things really get worse?

When U Ko Yin finally leaves, Araf breathes a big sigh of relief before wandering to the front of the shop to count the toy soldiers and check how many, if any, of his favorite toys have been sold.

"Hasina," her father calls out. He pulls out a tiffin tin with some lunch in it that he has saved for her. "Here you are." He places the food in front of her.

"Baba," she asks shyly, as she eats, "is it true, what U Ko Yin said about the helicopters? Do they mean war is coming?"

Her father knits his brow. "Things are changing in Myanmar. Change is always dangerous. You can go forward but you can also go backward. Sometimes at the same time."

Hasina recalls how hopeful some of the Rohingya men and women in the bazaar had been just last year, leading up to the election. After fifty years of a military government, people were finally able to vote! Others were skeptical that Aung San Suu Kyi would plead their cause. But then came the terrible blow when no Muslims were allowed to vote.

"Sit Tat fear weakness; they fear disunity and the break-up of the country. They wish for the old days."

"Will the country break up?"

Ibrahim shrugs. "Arakan was a kingdom for almost a thousand years before the British came. The Arakanese were ruled by the British for just over a hundred years and by Myanmar for only forty. The Arakanese are independent-minded. They have always wanted their kingdom returned. But now, they are frightened we Rohingya will want our own country too and will take theirs. After all, we have also been here for hundreds of years, no matter what the government claims."

"Is that what we want? Our own country?"

"We simply want the rights of full citizens. Medicine for your grandmother. School for you and Araf."

"The woman on the TV talked about ARSA. A Rohingya army."

"Hmph." Ibrahim makes a disapproving sound.

"Isak's cousin Jamaal says they are standing up for our people."

"Before ARSA was an army they were a group called Harakah al-Yaqin. They used to go around beating villagers who didn't say their prayers."

"Isak says—"

"Hasina, Sit Tat fight for a single nation. The Arakanese Army fight for an Arakanese nation.

ARSA fight for a Rohingya Muslim nation. But there are other Muslims. Where do they fit in?"

"And the Buddhists who want only Buddhists in Myanmar?"

Her father sighs. "If there are over one hundred and thirty-five ethnic groups in Myanmar, and many religions, then what happens if we all fight one another? Surely you can see that we are weaker separately than we are together?"

Hasina mulls over her father's words as she finishes her lunch. Is it true that violence leads to worse violence? Or is ARSA right to stand up for the Rohingya? She piles up the tiffin tins, ready to carry to the communal water trough at the front of the market, and calls out, "TV, Araf?"

When they have said goodbye, Hasina leaves Araf watching the TV set while she rinses the lunch tins clean outside at the water trough. A shadow falls over her, and she turns to see the kind man from earlier, the man who changed the TV channel.

Hasina lowers her face and hands in the polite *shi-kho*, as she did with U Ko Yin. The Arakanese man makes a slight and polite bow of the head back. He checks over his shoulder before speaking.

"I want to warn you," he says in Myanmar language. "You look like a respectable girl. The government is planning to drive away your people. We cannot control the bad behavior of our own people. You must be very careful."

Then he nods politely again and leaves.

CHAPTER 10

The stone that Hasina first felt in her belly the day the helicopters came never leaves her now. Weeks go by and still it weighs her down. No matter what she does, she cannot shake it. It is the heaviness of fear.

She is not the only one who feels this way. Heaviness is everywhere. Even the air above seems thick with helicopters, squads of them flying up and down the Arakanese sky, now as familiar as the mountains, yet still terrifying. Each time they fly over, her father or Isak tells her that a village or settlement has been attacked by Sit Tat soldiers in their deep green uniforms.

Police begin to patrol the streets of Teknadaung more frequently too. Jeeps of men and women wearing blue camouflage speed up and down the dirt roads of Eight Quarters. They unsettle Monu Mush, who bellows just before they arrive and doesn't stop until they are gone. Police march through the Rohingya part of the bazaar. They look for trouble, prodding truncheons into piles of *longyis* and knocking over tins of biscuits with their guns. Even U Ko Yin is unimpressed.

"Police are terrible for business."

"This is war," Aunt Rukiah rages in her madrassa, "the never-ending Arakanese War. Buddhist versus Muslim. Myanmar versus the state of Rakhine. And Arakanese and Burmese against Rohingya. They want us out. They want us dead."

Harvest comes. The rice crop is good. Men and women, knee deep in water, cut sheaves of rice, green stems heavy with yellow grain, and toss them onto dry land. Even Ghadiya joins them in the paddy field, her skirts hitched up. Araf chases the ducklings. A mother duck chases Araf back, pecking him on the legs.

"Serves you right," laughs Nurzamal. Her flock of sleek and healthy ducklings is larger than Sabikam Nahor's. She passes Araf a basket and tells him to hunt for eggs. He fills a basket with blue eggs.

"Look, Hasina, I found six!"

Hasina smiles at his perfect blue eggs. This is the first year that she is allowed to winnow the rice with the women. She is still learning the knack for sending the coarse seed grains high enough into the air so that the husk floats off and the grains rain down.

It is during the winnowing that the women talk.

"I hear they are looking for young men, men who might be in ARSA," whispers Rehana's mother. "I hear they cut them into pieces."

"I hear they are killing children, *babies*," whispers Aziza Begum.

"And doing worse things to young girls," whispers Rehana's mother.

"Shh," warns Aziza Begum, jutting her chin toward Hasina.

But it's too late. Hasina's mouth goes dry. She remembers Ghadiya's story about Rivka, the girl left under a *longyi* in an open field. She remembers how Isak's voice lifted when he spoke of ARSA on the day the helicopters came. The stone grows heavier.

After harvest, Nurzamal tells Hasina she must not walk along the main road anymore. Araf will be staying home. Nurzamal would prefer that Hasina stayed home too, but then who would take lunch to Baba? Could Baba come home? The stall is already losing money. Hasina begs, swears, promises she will be fine. She does not tell her mother that sometimes, when she flits past the Arakanese paddy fields, where the Arakanese families are also bringing in their rice, she hears the word *kalama* behind her. She burns with shame every time she hears it.

Ghadiya too feels the heaviness. Hasina often catches her biting her nails, staring into space and silently counting. One night, Hasina is woken by the sound of fumbling. On her side of the room, Ghadiya is putting things into her tattered orange bag.

"What are you doing?" Hasina whispers to her cousin.

"Nothing," Ghadiya snaps.

Worst of all are the nights Hasina and Ghadiya lie awake listening to their mothers quarreling.

"You must close the school. It attracts attention. You will bring the police down on us."

"And so, our girls learn nothing and know nothing? What will they do when they are grown women? How will they stand up for themselves?"

Hasina winces at her aunt's words, which seem designed to wound her mother. Her mother is a farmer's daughter—she cannot read or write. Yet Hasina would prefer the school to remain open. She would prefer to learn.

"Their husbands will do it for them." Nurzamal's voice is bitter, hurt. "A good husband takes care of his wife. A good husband doesn't run away."

"How dare you," Aunt Rukiah hisses. "Rashid sends us money and medicine. Rashid, a lawyer, working in a prawn factory, who pays bribes to do that menial job. It is Rashid who keeps this family afloat."

As always, Dadi Asmah ends the fights.

"Now, now, my daughters. The Arakanese Buddhists fight us, the government fights us, the police and the army too. Do we really need to fight among ourselves as well?"

Still, the peace at home is as uneasy as the peace in town.

Besides, there is truth to what Aunt Rukiah says. Hasina can see for herself that their family stall is doing poorly. So is the Brothers & Sons Puppet Stall. So are all of the Rohingya businesses. At the bazaar, Arakanese customers no longer wish to buy from Muslims. Here too Hasina hears the word *kalama* flung at her as she passes by.

The days grow hotter. At the bazaar, the TV is surrounded by a crowd of Arakanese and Rohingya men and women. Buddhist extremists in a big northern city are marching and shouting about how her people are Muslim intruders. A yelling match starts. A man shoves a woman. The police are called. Hasina knows this is how riots begin.

A few days later, when Hasina takes lunch to her father, there is a big empty space where the TV used to be.

"The men came and took it down," Isak tells her. "It's not just the cartoons we will miss. They don't want us to see what they've been doing to our people." He picks up Daamini, who is no longer a kitten but now an accomplished hunter, her blue eyes as deep as the Bay of Bengal. "Jamaal says the less we know, the worse things will get."

That afternoon, as Hasina sits with Ibrahim, the Rohingya part of the bazaar is hot, sleepy and empty. There are no shoppers browsing in the aisles. There have been no shoppers for days.

"Why did they take the TV, Baba?"

He sighs and wipes his face with his hand. "It is a way to control. No information, no warning. No information, no understanding."

Lately, Ibrahim looks defeated. He opens up earlier, stays open later. None of it makes any difference. The stall is doing worse. Hasina hates to see him so stressed. She works to spare him, dusts the stall, tidies his newspapers.

"Not that you could rely on the news they broadcast anyway," her father mutters, and Hasina remembers what Asmah says: They *are clever.* They *know how to sow dissension.*

The mysterious *they.* Hasina does not understand why *they* are so against her people. Are *they* the government? She asks her father.

Ibrahim takes a deep breath. "They are the government who wants to stay in power. They are the generals who want to keep their power and the riches they have made as the rulers of Myanmar. They are the extreme Buddhists who believe that Myanmar should be one religion only, and that religion is Buddhism. They are the Arakanese who want their own homeland and think we will take it from them. They are the UN and the NGOs who only watch and do not help us."

"So, why don't we fight like ARSA wants us to?"

"I do not wish for *you* to fight. I do not want to see *Araf* fight. I only wish to live. We want to live in our homes, to live our lives. How would fighting help us?"

Later, Hasina lies awake sifting through her father's explanation. It hurts to think of herself as second-class, in the same way that it hurts to be called *kalama.* It makes her feel small and insignificant. For what is a person without a home? Without a name?

As the weeks pass, Nurzamal worries more and more. The happy, carefree mother from the harvest has gone, the mother eaten up by worry returned.

The rains begin to fall, the air heavy and humid. One day, while Hasina is helping at the stall, there are more protests in town. Mobs gather. They parade up and down the main street, past the police station, past the International Aid office. They insist that foreigner aid organizations, who are biased toward Muslims, leave. Now. Her father shuts the roller door to the stall, and together, they hide in the back until they can make their way home after dark.

Nurzamal is waiting for them, crazed with fear. Tears mar her lovely face and she is shaking. She takes Hasina by the shoulders and shakes her until her teeth chatter.

Hasina is terrified to see her mother so wild. Her father pulls her from her mother's grip.

"Where were you?" Nurzamal demands.

"There were protests," Ibrahim explains wearily.

"I'm sorry, Mama," Hasina whispers.

"Stupid, stupid girl. A Rohingya is a target; a Rohingya girl is an easy target. You will not go to the bazaar anymore. Go to your room."

So Hasina stays home now. Her poor, worn-out baba must take his lunch in the mornings and eat it all alone. Cold rice. Cold fish curry.

It is on a heavy, gray morning just before Dhurh that her mother rushes into the madrassa holding a flat, shiny thing. "What is this?" she shouts.

The color drains from Aunt Rukiah's face. "Tara, Rosie, Aman, school is over for today. Please pack up your things. Quickly."

The three girls trade surprised looks as they gather

their books and pens. But before they have finished, the thing in Nurzamal's hand emits a loud shriek and, shocked at the sound, Nurzamal drops it. It falls to the floor with a tinkling thud.

"Oh no," Aunt Rukiah cries, "what have you done?" She snatches up the shiny thing. She smooths her hand over the cracked screen, her tears falling on the glass.

"What *is* it?" Tara whispers to the others.

"A hand phone," Ghadiya whispers back, her hands shaking. "It is how we talk to my father in Malaysia. He sent it to us."

A hand phone! Hasina can't believe her aunt has such a thing. Hand phones are illegal and if you are caught with one, the police take you in.

"You bring *that* into my house and ask me what *I* have done? How could you be so stupid!" Nurzamal roars.

The hand phone emits another shriek.

"Shush." Aunt Rukiah, distracted by the phone, dismisses Nurzamal's scolding with a wave of her hand. "Look at this, Babi," she says, using the family term for sister-in-law. Her face is stricken.

Aunt Rukiah holds the phone up for Nurzamal to see. All of them, Tara, Rosie, Aman, Ghadiya and Hasina, crowd around the shiny screen. There is a blue square of text that reads: *Going out today? Be careful! Muslim gangs are on the move. Stay safe, friends.*

Nurzamal gasps in horror.

"Wait." Aunt Rukiah swipes her thumb across the glass. Another message appears. *Going out today? Be careful! Buddhist gangs are on the move. Stay safe, friends.*

It is the same message—except for one thing.

Cold fear prickles Hasina's scalp. Why send the same message about different groups like that? What does it mean?

Just then, Dadi Asmah shuffles into the madrassa. "What is this shouting about?" Her voice is calm but firm.

"Your daughter has brought an illegal hand phone into this house," Nurzamal begins.

"Never mind that, look at this, Mama." Rukiah shows her mother the messages. Asmah takes a deep breath and sucks her teeth.

"But the Buddhists are already mad with us," Tara exclaims, her voice fearful. "What will happen when they see that?"

"They will be even madder," Asmah replies. "And so will the hotheads among our people. Whoever sent that message wishes the people of Rakhine to fight among ourselves. They will divide us to conquer us. The British did the same thing in their day."

Who sent the message? Hasina wonders. Who wins if everybody is fighting with everyone else? Who is *they*? The government? The Arakanese Army? Extreme Buddhists who want Myanmar to be of one religion? Sit Tat? ARSA?

And who will help people like her and her family? People who just want to live peacefully?

Hasina feels sick with fear, worn out by worry.

The day after Hasina's mother finds the hand phone, Aunt Rukiah closes the school. She bids a tearful farewell to Tara and Aman and Rosie. She packs up their books and gives them homework to get on with. But how will they do it all on their own?

"It's as if the Buddhists and the army have won and we helped them," she growls through her tears, and Ghadiya puts an arm around her shoulders.

"We will continue on our own," Aunt Rukiah tells Hasina and Ghadiya, drying her tears and trying to comfort them. "We will have our own school, just us."

Sadly, Hasina flicks through the pages of her math problems. The equilateral triangle, the square of a hypotenuse—that is as much as she will ever know about geometry. Despite Aunt Rukiah's promises, she fears that this is where her education will end. She wanted to finish the tenth standard like her father. To go to university, like her grandmother. But none of that is possible now.

Early in August, army and police flood into Teknadaung again. They stop men and boys, they stop women, they stop anyone they don't like the look of. They confiscate anything that might be used as a weapon. Housewives lose their fish knives, little boys their slingshots.

Nurzamal is out in her paddy field when she is approached by a man wearing a blue police uniform. He takes her *hasi*, the long, wide-bladed knife she uses to cut the weeds and trim the plants.

"Please, *Thakin*, but how am I supposed to plant without that?" she asks him.

She is body searched for her insolence.

"He touched me everywhere," she howls at Ibrahim, "everywhere."

Hasina and Ghadiya lie rigid in their beds listening to Nurzamal's rage at this humiliation. In the morning, she will not leave her bed. She refuses to go to the paddy field. She won't cook. She won't eat. Araf begs her to get up. Aunt Rukiah takes over in the kitchen.

Now, each morning when she wakes up, Hasina dreads what might happen that day. Nothing could be worse than this.

She is wrong.

Three weeks later, at the stroke of midnight, ARSA attacks police stations again, just as they did before. Their "soldiers" are farmers with slingshots and fishermen with sticks.

And after that, things get far worse.

CHAPTER 11

The men come at night, in trucks along the beach highway, and over the Rakhine Mountains in helicopters.

The first Hasina knows of it is her aunt's voice, urgent, full of fear. "Up, up. *Get up!*"

The second thing is smoke. *Fire!* Hasina thinks. She half-falls, half-rolls from her bed and lands hard on the floor, her arm under her. Where is the fire? There is light outside her window. But inside, all is dark. Is it day or night?

"Out, out. Get out of the house!" Then Aunt Rukiah is gone from the room.

Hasina grabs her *numal* out of instinct, wrapping it around her neck. She hears a thud as Ghadiya's feet hit the floor. They race down the hall together, Ghadiya limping and falling, Hasina's arm around her, until they reach the madrassa. Her father is there at the door to the garden, clasping Araf by the forearm. Araf is crying. Or is it Araf? Hasina can hear wails, but perhaps it is from somewhere in the house. Then there is a scream.

68

A voice snarling, angry, like an animal. Another. And another. Are they inside? Or outside? Is that her mother? Her grandmother?

Her father pushes Araf toward her. "Stay together. Hide. Stay alive. Take care of them, Hasina. I will come for you."

And then he shoves her out into the yard.

"Run," he shouts after them. "And *don't stop!*"

Hasina runs, half-dragging her cousin and her brother behind her. Is their house on fire? Is there a storm? Why is her father crying?

Outside of the compound, on Third Mile Street, she halts. Which way to go? All around is the stench of smoke—not wood burning, but plastic, meat, something horrible. Now that they are standing in the road, Hasina realizes that she is still in sleeping clothes. Should she go back inside and change?

Bewildered, she looks around her. Above, nothing but stars. To the left, nothing but the forest and paddy fields and the river running in the dark night. But behind her, down the highway end of Third Mile Street, nothing is as she knows it.

A man stands with a hose that breathes fire, which licks up the fences, along the walls of houses, and snakes through the vegetable gardens so that there are now huge flames where only this morning were her neighbors' homes. And in the firelight, figures move. Firelight shines on the blades of their long *suri*. Firelight picks out the glitter of their eyes. Men or demons? She cannot say.

There is rain too. She feels it whizzing past her. But is

it rain or something lethal? What to do? All she can think is, *Run, we must run.* But which way? She knows, only by instinct, that these men or demons have come from the open ground where she used to play soccer. Which means there is only one way to go.

"The river. The Lower Forest," Hasina gasps. "Quickly."

She swings Araf onto her back and hurls herself straight toward the river.

Her plan is simple. Run. Get Araf and Ghadiya to the forest. Hide there. Wait for her father and mother and grandmother to find them. But she, the fastest of the girls on the soccer pitch, feels like she is wading through mud. Ghadiya's limp slows her down and Araf's weight drags on her. *Run*, she tells herself. *Don't stop*, she tells herself.

All around them, their neighbors are also running or wailing or standing holding each other. Old men, small children, mothers with babies. Mothers screaming *for* their babies. Hasina keeps moving, though her chest aches. Her father said *don't stop*. So she does not stop, and she does not let Ghadiya stop either.

When they're almost at the standpipe at the end of Third Mile Street, almost to where the little path leads left to the Lower Forest on their side of the river, Ghadiya tugs at Hasina's arm, drags her to the side of the road into the long grass.

"Shh! Look. Men."

At the standpipe, shadowy figures merge in the flickering firelight. Men or demons? These men seem calm, murmuring to each other. Hasina slides Araf from her shoulder and pulls him into the clumps of grass beside the road.

That stone is in her belly again, heavier and harder than ever. How will she run, how will she keep moving, how will she get them all away and into a hiding place with this stone inside her? Maybe she should stop running. Maybe they should stay here. Hope that these are men and not demons. They cannot get past them anyway. Why not just give up?

The three men are speaking in Burmese. There's a flare as they light their torches, and their faces glow orange. One of them gestures down Third Mile Street and then toward the Lower Forest, curving his arm around as if giving directions to Fourth Mile, the next street along.

The leader heads along the raised path toward the Lower Forest, while the other two turn back toward Third Mile Street. Hasina fuses herself to the ground, shrinking from the torchlight. And then all is dark around the water-pump.

Has her father run from their house? Has her mother hidden? Her grandmother? Her aunt? Hasina realizes that these men are not using the torches for light alone—they mean to burn the houses at the top of Third Mile Street.

Should she run back home, warn them that the men are coming? If she does, can she be sure Ghadiya and Araf will be safe here without her? Ghadiya, whose chest is heaving with every breath. Araf, whose teeth chatter with terror. *Run*, her father said. *Stay together. Hide.*

Precious seconds pass.

Like the morning the helicopters came, the answer comes as an image. Pontoons, floating on the Farak River.

"We need to cross the river," she whispers. "We need to cross the Children's Bridge."

But even as she says it, the thought of crossing the river fills her with dread. In the dark, it would be so easy to miss a step and slide into that deep, fast water. And these men, with their demon eyes, if they see her climbing down to the river, would they not follow?

"I don't want to," Araf cries. "I am tired."

"Araf, Baba and Mama said we must. We're going to take baby steps. First, we're going to the river. Then, we're going to cross together. All right?"

"All right," Ghadiya whispers.

"Carry me," Araf demands.

"I will carry you, but you must not make a sound."

First Ghadiya moves onto the road. Keeping crouched and low, she hurries to the standpipe and then across the dirt path and down over the top of the river-bank to the water below. Hasina waits for a minute after she disappears. No one comes. It is safe to go.

"All right, Araf, climb up."

Together, Hasina and Araf scuttle along the side of the road. They reach the standpipe, cross the path and then drop down into the damp, cool darkness beside the river. Hasina lets Araf down from her back and half-scrambles, half-falls down the bank.

"Ghadiya?" she whispers.

"I am here," comes the reply.

"Araf?"

Nothing. Fear stabs at Hasina's ribs. Has he fallen into the river as she almost did? Wouldn't she have heard the splash?

"Araf?" she whispers, this time a little louder.

"Shh. You said we must not make a sound!" Araf's small voice comes from behind her. Hasina sighs her relief into the darkness. Safe. They are almost safe.

Now that her eyes have adjusted, she can just make out the posts of the pontoon. She leads them down to the water.

The river is black. The water is flowing fast; she can hear it. One small slip, and the current will sweep them away with no chance of rescue. Suddenly her plan seems foolish. They should wait until light. They should go back.

She thinks about the men, their faces, the bright flames of their torches, and knows they cannot go back. She steadies herself. *Think about the goal. Think about that rectangle.*

Hasina puts one hand on the railing and finds the guide rope, then puts a foot onto the pontoon. It sinks beneath her weight, water oozing up over the raft and gleaming silver in the night. She takes a deep breath and puts her second foot onto the bridge. Immediately, she can feel the river current beneath her feet, pushing back. The power of all that water, water leaking over her sandals, making the deck slippery. What if they fall in?

What if Araf falls in? How will she face her mother? She grips the rope more firmly. "Okay, Araf," she whispers, "take my hand."

But when Araf is on the pontoon, it is he who leads her. "Baby steps," he whispers and that is what they take, sliding their feet a little bit forward each time until they reach the end of the raft. Then, a step into the dark and onto the next raft. Again, it is Araf who leads her until they are safe on the other side.

"Stay here, don't move," she tells him.

"Okay," he whispers.

Now she's back at the opposite bank, reaching for her cousin's trembling hand.

If it is too difficult for Ghadiya to balance in the light of day, how will it be in the dark? Ghadiya puts one foot onto the pontoon and it sinks beneath their combined weight. She pulls back from Hasina and nearly falls into the water, but lands on her bottom.

"I can't," Ghadiya whimpers, tears falling in silver tracks down her face. "I can't do it."

"You can."

"I can't. I will drop my bag." Hasina can just make out the orange Shan bag slung over Ghadiya's shoulder.

"Please, Ghadiya!"

"Leave me here. I'll be okay, Baba," her cousin sobs.

Baba? Hasina peers at her cousin. Is this what happened when Rashid left? Did he try to take them too? If Ghadiya is seeing ghosts, how will she get her across?

Then Hasina has a brainwave. "What if we crawl?

Like this." She drops to her hands and knees. Water oozes around her wrists, but with her weight more evenly distributed, there is little motion on the pontoon. She slides one knee forward. The raft doesn't budge.

"Look, Ghadiya, can you do it this way?"

"I have a better idea," her cousin cries. "Come, help me down."

Hasina helps Ghadiya onto the pontoon. Instead of crawling on hands and knees, Ghadiya sits and shuffles like a crab. At the gap between the rafts, she drops onto her side and heaves herself across. Then it is back onto her bottom, and at last she's on the other bank.

Finally, it is Hasina's turn to cross on her hands and knees, and together they scramble to the top of the riverbank.

Hasina lies panting on the bank gathering herself. The stars above are cold and distant and very beautiful. Beyond a few paddy fields the darker patch of the High Forest rises into the night. If they can climb into the High Forest, they will be safe from the men like demons. Hasina looks across the water at the home she has lived in all her life. The street is alight. Even though the fires are far, Hasina can feel their heat on her face, see their glow on the faces of her brother and cousin.

"What are we going to do?" Ghadiya asks.

All Hasina has are her father's words. "We are going to stay together. We are going to hide. We are going to wait for Baba to find us all."

Is her father even safe? And her mother, her grandmother, her aunt? She can't think about that now. All she can do is what she's been asked to do. *Run. Stay together. Hide.*

"Come on," she says. "We're going to hide in the High Forest."

"I'm scared." Araf's voice is trembling.

"I'm scared too," Ghadiya admits.

"Baba will come in the morning," Hasina comforts them. "He said he will, so he will."

"Carry me," Araf begs. His voice is tiny. Hasina feels tiny inside too. Aching and fearful.

"Ready?" She hoists Araf onto her back, takes Ghadiya by the hand, and the three of them walk quickly toward the darkness of the High Forest.

CHAPTER 12

The High Forest is dark and hot, the air sticky.
Strange sounds drift from the treetops. Thick vines catch
at her feet and biting insects run along her arms and
face. But Hasina knows that on the other side of the river
things are far worse.

She stumbles with Araf into a hollow beneath a teak
tree, Ghadiya right behind them. This is where they will
rest tonight. She lays Araf on the ground, then settles
herself next to him, Ghadiya on the other side. Hasina
unfurls the *numal* from her head and gently spreads it
over them, like a blanket. Throughout it all, her heart is
beating so loud, so fast in her chest, she thinks that those
men with demon eyes must be able to hear it all the way
across the river. Like a summons, or a beacon.

They soothe Araf to sleep and then talk in hushed
whispers of what they have seen.

"Those men were soldiers," Ghadiya says.

"But they didn't have uniforms."

"In the south, men came in the afternoon. We saw

their trucks rolling into town—they raised a big cloud of dust. They had knives and clubs and sticks. They wore red bandanas to cover their faces—they didn't have uniforms, but they all looked the same. Like the army looks the same." Ghadiya pauses, remembering. "Baba was sad and scared just before the men came to town. He said they would be coming for the people like him—lawyers, journalists. And that we would have to run. He left that day."

So that is what happened to Uncle Rashid—an attack like this one. Did that mean her parents would also have to run? What would happen to the three of them then?

Ghadiya's voice takes on a dreamy quality. "Baba was right—the men did come. They came that night. These were not army, they were police. They pounded on the door so hard, I thought it would break. Mama shoved me into the linen cupboard."

Hasina shivered. Poor Ghadiya in the cupboard.

"I heard them talking. I heard her say no, no, no. And then, I hear this noise like a dog whimpering. When they were gone, I found my mother on the floor. She was covered in blood. And that is when we left."

Hasina is frozen in horror. Poor Aunt Rukiah. Poor Ghadiya. And now, it was happening again. This time to her family as well.

"Do you think my mama is with your father and mother?"

"Yes, I think so."

"I'm sorry I was so scared on the bridge." Ghadiya's voice breaks. "Thank you," she sobs, "thank you for not leaving me behind."

"You were brave, Ghadiya, to cross like that."

"Not as brave as you."

They talk on until Ghadiya just stops. Hasina knows that she has fallen asleep. Now she is all on her own in the dark night.

Brave? She does not feel brave. She feels weak, and terrified, with no idea about what she should do next. Every forest sound makes her start. A snap of a twig means the men are here, coming for them. A gleam of moonlight on the broad face of a leaf is the blade of a knife shining in the night. What would the men do to them if they come? She thinks of Ghadiya's story, of what happened to Aunt Rukiah. What does it feel like, to be beaten like that?

For hours, Hasina's heart continues to pound and her mind races. Why *did* the men come? What did they want? Why are they burning houses? Is it a punishment? What has her family done? Where is her father? Her mother? Her aunt? Her grandmother? What has happened to their house? Their neighbors? Tara? Isak? When will her father come for them, as he promised? Tonight? And then, her mind turns back to the start and the questions whirl through it all over again. She cannot think of answers. Nothing makes any sense.

❖❖

She blinks her eyes against the brightness. It is already light. What happened to the call to Fagr from the clock? She should have been up ages ago to get water. Why are there tree branches in her room? And what or who is squeezing her like a rice cake?

Hasina wriggles free and raises herself onto an elbow. Araf has rolled himself into a little ball and is curled against her stomach. When she moves, he just burrows in tighter. That explains the squeezing.

The memory of the night before returns with full force, her father's desperate words: *Take care of them, Hasina. Stay together. I will find you.*

Hasina sits up and looks around. The sound of his voice is so clear in her head, she thought he was here.

Her heartbeat rises and her body twitches with nervous energy as more of the night comes back to her. Sleep. She wishes she could sleep more, like Araf and Ghadiya. She leans back against the tree and closes her eyes. Takes a deep breath. Tries to calm herself.

But sleep is impossible. Behind her eyelids is fire.

CHAPTER 13

"Hasina, I am hungry.

"I am tired.

"I want my toys.

"I want Mama.

"I want Baba."

"He's coming," Hasina soothes Araf. "Be patient."

And then, the same refrain again. And again. And again. As persistent as the mosquitoes that whine in Hasina's ears.

The sun rises in the sky and dawn turns into morning. They have not eaten. What is there to eat? They have not drunk. What is there to drink? They pass the time waiting for Baba. They take it in turns, she and Ghadiya, to persuade Araf to be quiet. What if the men like demons come? What if ogres are near? Or tigers?

They try wheedling, cuddling him. Hasina tries bossing him and promising him all manner of things—rice cakes, toy soldiers, chewing gum, soft drink. But

Araf is not listening. He wriggles. He whines and cries. Hasina, frustrated, raises her own voice. "Be *quiet!*"

Her shout echoes around the forest. Visions of the men like demons bounce around her head. What if they heard her? Hasina waits for the sound of their boots, the gleam of their knives.

Nobody comes.

Soon enough, Araf begins again. Fidgeting, wriggling, annoying. Ghadiya too is sulky, and won't stay quiet about what her father has done, or her mother. Or what she would do if things were up to her. Like go outside and find some food. Or water at least. Or somewhere bigger or better or just somewhere else.

Finally, Hasina can't stand it any longer. "I will go out; I will see if it is safe. I will see if I can find food or water. You two stay here."

"Thanks a lot," Ghadiya complains, "for leaving me with him."

"Araf, you behave. Or ..."

"Or what?"

Or what is a good question. Or she won't come back? That is what she is hoping will not happen. "Or Baba will be very cross with you when he comes, and you won't get a soft drink."

"Soft drink," Araf mutters. "Cola, lemonade, orange fizz. I want all three."

"Shh."

Hasina creeps out of the hollow. The light through the leaves is mottled, the air still cool. She stands, stretches, unkinking her body after the long, damp hours squished together under the tree. It feels good and her anger disappears—leaving only fear. She wills herself to be calm, forces herself to listen for the sound of movement, sniffs the air for the smell of the men, of burning or sweat.

Nothing.

She looks back at the thicket. She cannot see a thing. Only now she realizes that they have been very lucky. They found a hollow space beneath the thick, leafy branches of a tall teak tree, and they are completely hidden.

But are they safe?

She remembers a story Asmah used to tell. *In the emerald forest, the tiger circles his prey.* Are there tigers in this wood?

Hasina swallows hard. *There are no tigers here,* she tells herself. *Or ogres.*

But she could be the tiger. *Think like a tiger. Circle the hollow like a tiger. Make sure all is safe.*

She will need a landmark, so that she can find the hollow again. The High Forest vegetation is thicker than that of the Lower Forest. Three steps over is a *sein pan* or golden mohur tree—flame of the forest, with its orange flowers. She could take her bearings from that. Hasina estimates the distance between their teak tree hideout and the flame tree. This will be her radius.

Scooping up a handful of flowers, she moves forward, in a circle, with their teak tree at its center. She creeps along, her body tense, ready to run, dropping a flower every four or five steps. The ground is rough under her bare feet. Before each step, she looks for scorpions and snakes and centipedes.

When she completes the circle, she knows there are no tigers and no demon men nearby. Or others hiding like them. They are on their own.

Hasina relaxes and sighs as she rolls her head and shoulders. She listens to what the forest is telling her. There is not a single bird in the air, but there is the sound of wind—and something else. Is it water? Not the river, but a stream.

Suddenly, Hasina is desperately thirsty. She picks up another handful of flowers and sets off, following that sound.

By the time she has dropped ten flowers, the forest opens out into a clearing. Through this runs a *chaung*, a small stream. She looks for the round burps of groundwater emerging from its bed. Then she drinks as if she will never stop.

Nothing is as delicious as that sweet stream water.

Hasina dips the end of her *numal* into the stream and wipes her face, her hands, the back of her neck. She stretches out across a flat rock and closes her eyes.

The question now is, what to do next? Baba said to wait. So they will wait. But for how long? Another problem occurs to her. How will Baba find them when they are so well hidden?

With a shake, Hasina stops herself from thinking about it. First things first, as Asmah says. And the first thing is to find her way back to the others so they too can have a drink. Maybe she can find something to take water back? She circles the stream again, wider and wider, like a tiger. Then she follows the water.

The stream is clear across the rocks, but as she follows it into the woods it gets deeper and faster. She can see runs all the way to the cliffs and waterfalls that spill into the Farak upstream.

Ouch! Her toe hits something hard. She bends and rubs her foot. In the dirt is an old beer bottle, half-buried. So people did come here. People who drank beer. But they aren't here now. She drops to her knees and digs up the bottle, rinsing it clear in the stream.

In another ten minutes, she finds herself back at the groundwater bubbles. She fills the bottle, then turns and retraces her steps to the hollow where Araf and Ghadiya are waiting.

"You move over."

"No. *You* move over."

"NO. YOU. MOVE. OVER!"

Hasina cannot believe her ears. Ghadiya and Araf are quarreling at the tops of their voices! How is she supposed to keep them safe if they go on like this? White fury fills her. She will teach them a lesson.

Slowly she creeps forward, then yanks aside the fringe of branches. "*Grrr!*"

Ghadiya shrieks and Araf bursts into tears. *Stupid girl*, Hasina admonishes herself.

It takes a while to calm them down, and then they wait just to be sure no one has heard them. Finally, when they have finished the spring water from the bottle, she takes them back to the stream, flower by flower.

She shows Araf the spot where the bubbles come to the surface. He puts his whole head into the stream. Then it is Ghadiya's turn. Then it is her own.

"Come here, Araf." She washes his face with her *numal*.

"Ouch, stop it!"

She grins at him. "So, it is a boy under there, not some wild animal."

"Grrr," he replies, his little hands made into monster claws. Then he stops. "Hina, who were those men?"

Hasina sits back on the rocks. She too wonders who the demon men are. They did not wear uniforms. "I am not sure, Araf."

"They were army, for sure," Ghadiya avers. "Just like the men who came for my father."

"What have they done with Mama?" Araf asks, his voice tiny.

"Baba will protect Mama."

"And Dadi too?"

"And Dadi too."

"And my mama?" Ghadiya asks, her voice also tiny.

"Your mama too, I am sure of it. He was awake in time to save us, so we know he will have taken care of them." Hasina makes sure her voice sounds confident, although she doesn't feel it.

For the rest of the afternoon, they sit beside the stream. Araf wades in the shallows. Ghadiya limps to a deep brown pool where she drags her *numal* through the water.

Hasina thinks about what to do next. They cannot stay here indefinitely. There is no food. And even though there is water, she knows very well that water like this soon causes sickness.

Besides, like Araf and Ghadiya, she is desperate to know what has happened to her family.

But she is also afraid to go back, afraid of what she will find. With a shiver she remembers the demon men and their torches. The screams of her neighbors.

Suddenly, there is a shriek from Ghadiya. "Look!"

Ghadiya holds her *numal* open to reveal two fat gray river prawns, still squirming. Hasina could shout with happiness. Prawns! Prawns mean lunch.

Hasina and Ghadiya use their *numals* twisted across hastily tied frames of bamboo to fish out more prawns. When they have five of them, Hasina starts a small fire using the glass bottle and bark and kindling Araf has gathered. In no time, a cheery little cooking fire is going.

Hasina, Ghadiya and Araf splay the fat prawns on sticks, wrapped in pennywort leaves, and roast them over the coals, fanning the flames to keep the smoke down. Soon, the aroma of cooking flesh drifts upward, making their mouths water.

If the water was delicious, the prawns are even more so. They eat them straight from the leaves.

Sweet juice runs down Hasina's mouth and along her fingers. She crunches through the shells, licking her fingers and relishing each bite. If not full, at least they are no longer ravenous. Hasina lies back on the warm rocks.

"When do you think Baba will come for us?" Araf asks.

"Soon, I am sure." She keeps her voice light, but she isn't at all sure that Baba will find them today.

She thinks about the hollow, and how it was only a few steps before she lost sight of it in the undergrowth. How would Baba find it? But how could they stay safe in plain sight? She doesn't know the answer. And now, the afternoon shadows are getting longer.

"How long will we have to stay in the forest?" Araf persists.

"I don't know," Hasina replies.

"Maybe they ran away."

Thanks a lot, Ghadiya, Hasina thinks. *Not helpful.* She stands up. "If Baba doesn't come today, we will just spend another night under the teak tree."

"Make him come!" Araf insists.

"How about we walk downstream to the cliffs? We might be able to see across the river."

"Let's go," Ghadiya cries, limping ahead.

They pick their way along the stream until they reach the cliffs. Here, the stream shoots down a rock face into a dark pool. Far below, the Farak River churns. Through the trees, all they can see of Third Mile Street is a plume of smoke.

For a long time they watch the stream flowing into the waterfall that cascades into the foaming pool below. When the light starts to fade, and they turn for the hollow, Hasina leans over for a last look. Suddenly she sees a swimmer, his arms trailing lazily through the water. She is about to wave to him, to shout out that they need help, when she realizes that this man isn't swimming. He is dead, his body carried along by the current.

CHAPTER 14

"Where is Baba?"

Araf's voice is high-pitched. Loud. Whiny. It hurts the ears. It makes the hot space of the hollow hotter, smaller, darker.

"Why hasn't he come?"

It has been two nights and one full day now. Each day, they are weaker. Each morning, Hasina is woken by hunger. Her belly doesn't rumble with just hunger either. She fears illness.

They are dirty and damp. When she rushed from her home two nights ago, she was barefoot in pajamas. How much longer will she have to go around undressed like this? It makes her feel naked and vulnerable.

And there is the sheer boredom of hanging around the forest. Of wondering if anyone else is hiding nearby. Of being careful, of forgetting to be careful, and then, with a jolt of fear, remembering to be careful all over again.

We are in an impossible position, Hasina thinks. *If we*

stay here much longer, we will get sick or starve. But if we go? With a shudder she remembers the men with eyes like demons.

So when Araf whines, again, "Where is Baba? Why hasn't he come?" Hasina wants to scream at him in frustration. She would like to know the answer too.

Ghadiya isn't helping. This morning, when Araf asked, "Where's Baba?" for the fifteenth time, she growled, "*My* father had to run away."

Hasina had to use all her willpower to not yell at her cousin, not to speak sharply, but to softly say, "Our Baba will come. He's just been held up."

But by mid-morning, as they sit beside the stream, Hasina is out of willpower.

"Where is Baba?" Araf whines.

"Coming," Ghadiya mocks, sarcastically. Hasina can feel her temper rising.

"Araf, go see if there are prawns in the pool," Hasina orders, and Araf trots off.

"If Baba says he'll find us, then he will find us," Hasina insists.

"My Baba said he'd find us too." Ghadiya's voice is sulky.

This is when Hasina loses it. Why does it all have to be up to her? "Not all Babas run away," she snarls. "Not all Babas leave their children. Some stay, no matter what."

Ghadiya's face crumples, and instantly Hasina regrets her words. "Sorry. Your father is a good man."

Ghadiya wipes away her tears. "He *is* a good man."

She hangs her head, stares at her fingers. "The day the men came, it wasn't just my father who went to catch the boat. It was all three of us." Ghadiya's voice takes on that remembering quality again. "The boat engine was already going when we got to the docks. The captain threw a plank to shore for us. It was high up over the water. All the people on the deck were shouting, 'Hurry, hurry.'"

She pauses.

"I couldn't cross the plank. I froze. Father took this bag." Ghadiya unhooks the orange Shan bag from her shoulder. "He looped the strap around my body to hold me as he backed over the plank.

"But the boat jumped. I fell back onto shore. He fell in the water. A woman pulled him onto the boat and the captain dragged in the plank. Father begged them to wait.

"If I had crossed that plank, my mother would not have been beaten. My family would still be together."

Hasina's insides clamp with pity for her cousin. "You were only a little girl."

Ghadiya shrugs. "Maybe Uncle Ibrahim will come. But maybe he can't." She stands up and hooks her father's orange bag across her body. "Maybe we have to decide what to do for ourselves." She limps to the pool where Araf is searching for prawns.

Hasina turns over Ghadiya's story in her mind. Her cousin has a point. *What if something has happened to* Baba? She has another thought. What if he went to the Lower Forest? He would not know that the men at the standpipe had forced them across the river to the High Forest. It could take ages for him to find them.

She gathers the others. "I think we need to find out more about what is happening in Teknadaung. Soon."

"How?" Araf demands.

Hasina glances at her cousin. "I could go to the bazaar. I'd be sure to hear news there."

"It will be dangerous," Ghadiya says.

It would be risky. And the thought of coming up against those demon-eyed men again makes her feel icy inside. But she doesn't feel as if she has much choice.

"I will be careful. I won't wear my *numal*." Hasina feels a pang at going bareheaded. She has always resented wearing her *numal*. Now it feels like she is leaving something of herself behind.

"I will come to protect you," Araf insists.

Ghadiya rolls her eyes. *As if.* But for once, Hasina is ready. "If you come with me, who will be here waiting for Baba if he comes?"

"Ghadiya will," he counters.

"True. But Baba will be bringing breakfast."

"Breakfast?" Araf says, thinking it over.

"And soft drinks …"

"Soft drinks! I will stay here."

Hasina speeds across the paddy fields, her belly empty, her heart pounding. If things go well, she might find that the men with demon eyes have gone, that they can go home. If things go really, really well, she might even find Baba at the stall. And he might tell her that Mama and Dadi and Aunt Rukiah are safe at home, that most of what she saw was a nightmare. But if things go badly … well, she won't think about things going badly.

The sun on her face is much warmer here in the open. But it is good to be walking in their fields.

She drops down from the rocky forest path to the soft, sandy laneway through the Arakanese rice fields. She keeps low. But there is no one to see her. Not a single farmer is out. She runs past the Basic Education School. The gates are closed. No students are gathered in the yard. At the bazaar, the door is shuttered. Never before have the doors been closed during trading hours.

Hasina shrinks against the bazaar wall. What should she do? Maybe the back door is open. She creeps around the corner of the bazaar. A soldier stands before her. A soldier with a gun.

Hasina freezes.

The soldier has not noticed her. He is too busy searching through the piles of boxes, discarded from the bazaar. He is absorbed in this task, gingerly using the barrel tip of his rifle to poke into the pile, shifting the boxes apart.

Hasina can tell the soldier is afraid. That he is concentrating out of fear. A week ago, before the men came, there were those stories about explosions and bombs at police stations. Is that why the soldier is here now?

If she backs away slowly around the corner, he might not see her.

Silently, Hasina takes a step back, then another, her

eyes trained on the soldier. She puts a hand out to the corner of the building. But this time she puts her foot down on something sharp, something that pierces her foot. Something that hurts so much she cannot stifle a cry of pain.

The soldier's head whips up, and along with it the barrel of his gun. It's pointed at her heart. His dark eyes, behind the gunsight, lock on to hers. Those eyes are wide with fear.

There they are, Hasina and the soldier, like a cobra and a mouse. Each one convinced that they are the mouse and that the other is the cobra.

The soldier wears a green uniform with a red scarf and red badge. *Sit Tat.* But he is young, only a few years older than she is. Maybe that is why he looks so frightened. And so confused.

The soldier shoots a glance behind him. Hasina follows his gaze. Beyond the bazaar is a line of olive-green trucks. Is that where he came from? She can't see any other soldiers there.

He turns his face back to her. His expression is still confused, but something else is in his eyes. Pity. And sorrow.

From behind the bazaar, Hasina hears a voice. Loud, gruff, shouting orders in Burmese. The young soldier's eyes widen again in alarm. He jabs his chin to the right, pointing back the way she came. "Go," he hisses. "Run!"

CHAPTER 15

Hasina runs. She bolts from the bazaar as fast as she can, limping on her painful foot. She rounds the corner of the school at speed, and sprints down the deserted main street.

She doesn't stop until she comes to the paddy field where she ducks into the first ditch, head down.

She waits and waits, half-submerged in water. Her foot throbs and her brain swirls. She listens for the sound of boots running. Of that harsh voice barking in Burmese. *Round them up. Round them all up.*

Is this what happened to Baba? Did he meet a Sit Tat soldier on the way to find them? As she lies panting, Hasina realizes the risk of leaving the forest is too great. But that they need information more than ever.

Only once the sun has passed far to the west does she risk raising her head above the ditch. No one is in sight. She breathes a deep sigh of relief and hauls herself from the water to limp back to the forest.

In the hollow, as she wraps a strip of her *numal* around her foot, Hasina tells Ghadiya and Araf about the soldier, the trucks, the angry voice shouting in Burmese.

"I think he said, 'Round them up, all of them.'" What she doesn't tell them is how terrified she was to know that she is one of *them*. Someone to be rounded up. And so is Ghadiya, and Araf. Her mother's words on the day of the protest return to her. *You are a Rohingya.*

Ghadiya has an explanation. "First, it was the men that came to my town. Men like the demons we saw in Third Mile Street. Then it was the police. They came for my father, but he'd gone by then." She gives Hasina a look. It was the police, then, who beat Aunt Rukiah.

"Finally, it was the soldiers. We saw them when we were hiding alongside the road. For days we saw their trucks driving past. Mama made us leave the road then. She didn't want the soldiers to find us."

With a shiver, Hasina remembers the rough voice, the cruelty in it, and the young soldier's face. The way he too was afraid when he heard that barking voice. She would not like to meet any more soldiers. Not if she can help it.

But what Ghadiya said makes sense and gives her a tiny glimmer of hope. The soldiers closed the bazaar. That is why it was surrounded by their trucks. The soldiers may have prevented Baba from coming, just by being there. Which surely means that when the trucks leave, Baba will come. When the trucks are gone, they can go home again, although Hasina is frightened by what they might find.

But how will they know that the trucks have gone?

Hasina gazes up at the teak tree behind their hollow. It is tall, and on a hill. "If I can climb to the top of the tree, I should be able to see right across Teknadaung—"

"Which means you will be able to see if the trucks are there or gone," Ghadiya finishes.

"Right," says Hasina, although she is a bit annoyed at Ghadiya for finishing her sentence.

"*I* want to climb the tree," says Araf.

"Too dangerous," Hasina replies.

But with her injured foot, she finds she cannot climb the tree. Araf gets his way. She watches him, her heart in her mouth, as he hauls himself upward, branch after branch, hand over teeny hand.

Araf calls down that he sees the trucks. Lines of them near the bazaar. He sees them in Third Mile Street too. He isn't able to count them, but he sees "many many."

Many many trucks. The three of them settle into their hollow to talk over what that might mean.

"I think there must be soldiers all over town," Hasina says.

Ghadiya agrees, and the three of them decide that when the trucks are gone, it will be safe for Baba to come.

Over the next few days, the sky clouds over and rain falls in bursts. In between showers, Araf climbs to the top of the teak tree and scouts for trucks.

On their fifth morning in the forest, Araf calls down, "Not so many trucks." When he returns to the ground, he has a big grin on his face. The trucks are leaving. The soldiers are going. Baba will be coming. Finally, they will go home.

Later that morning, Araf climbs the tree again and sees the trucks turning onto the beach highway. By the early afternoon, they are all gone. The shadows grow longer, and still Baba does not come.

Will they have to spend another night in the hollow? At the thought of this, Hasina feels despair. She turns to the others. "Baba hasn't come, but the trucks have gone. If we don't go home now, we spend another night in the hollow. If we *do* go home ..."

"Can we just go?" Ghadiya begs. "Please, Hasina?"

Never before has Ghadiya spoken to her like this. It is as if she is the married woman already, the wife, the mother, the responsible one, when really, she is just Hasina, a girl only a year older than Ghadiya. Why can't they just go home? And with that realization, another one comes.

What Baba promised was for a time that is already in the past. Both Ghadiya and Araf are looking at her, watching for what she will say, because it *is* up to *her*. They are *her* responsibility now. She has to decide.

"Okay. Let's go home."

Is it the right thing to say? Just saying the words makes her feel better. They are going home. No more waiting.

But again Hasina's heart clenches with fear. What will they find there?

There is only one way to find out. Hasina winds her *numal*, tattered and dirty, around her hair. She has fished with it at the stream, used it as a blanket and a dressing. Ghadiya picks up her orange bag. Nothing remains of them in the hollow except the patches of flattened leaves where they slept, Hasina on the left, Ghadiya on the right, and Araf snuggled in between.

"Ready?"

"Ready." Ghadiya nods.

"Goodbye, hollow." Araf waves his little hand at the campsite.

"Yeah," adds Ghadiya, "thanks for everything."

Suddenly, Hasina feels sad to be leaving the hollow. It has been cool when it needed to be cool, warm when it needed to be warm, dry too. It has kept them hidden. It has kept them safe.

Now it is time to go home. But to what, she does not know.

CHAPTER 16

Hasina walks out of the mottled shade of the forest and into a gray afternoon. She helps Ghadiya clamber down the rocky path. She holds Araf's hand as they pick their way along the raised sandy path across the Arakanese paddy fields.

Just like on the day she met the soldier at the bazaar, the paddy fields are empty. There are no children on their way home from school. Even the birds and dogs are silent. Still, Hasina moves carefully and speaks in a low tone. Ghadiya and Araf follow her lead, frightened of breaking the silence.

At the riverbank, they make quick work crossing the Children's Bridge. Hasina's spirits lift a little. Araf first, tripping across the pontoons on light feet, turning to splash them. Araf, so naughty, so predictable! Ghadiya second, shuffling on her bottom, like a crab. Hasina, bringing up the rear.

With each step, she feels eager to get home one moment, uneasy at what they might find the next. Baba and Mama didn't come to find them. But there could be good reasons for that, couldn't there?

At last they are approaching the corner of Third Mile Street.

"What has happened to the pump?" Araf asks in a small voice.

The standpipe is broken. Not just broken, but smashed. The handle is splintered near the fulcrum, the broken bit of metal tossed to one side. All that is left is a tiny stub of the handle, impossible to pump. The spout is pinched flat.

"The men did that." Ghadiya's voice is flat.

"I'm thirsty," says Araf.

"So am I," says Ghadiya.

Hasina is too. Just looking at the standpipe makes her thirsty. "We'll get a drink at home from the *chatty* pot."

Still Araf and Ghadiya stand staring at the pump. "Come *on*," Hasina says.

But when they turn onto Third Mile Street, she cannot believe her eyes. The street where she has lived all her life, that she knows like the back of her hand, is almost unrecognizable.

Where there were houses standing close together, there is now mostly sky. Where there were rambling gardens, full of chickens and ducks and vines and herbs and fruit trees, there are only blackened sticks and brown leaves. Even the air is different. Heavy as the stone in her belly and stinking of smoke. It catches in her throat, choking her and making her eyes water.

Hasina stands taking it all in for a long moment,

wiping her eyes, Ghadiya and Araf rooted to the spot beside her. Eventually Hasina shakes herself, forcing her legs to move forward, forcing one foot in front of the other. "Come on," she says to the others.

Araf slips his little hand into hers. Then Ghadiya does the same, and they start along Third Mile.

No one speaks. All they can do is walk and look. So much has changed, it is hard to take it all in.

A wall standing on its own is all that remains of a bamboo house. On the other side of the street, a chimney has nothing around it. Ahead, a house is missing its roof. How will it keep dry when the rains come? To the left, an entire roof of corrugated metal lies crumpled on the ground. Scattered across the road are ordinary things, like cooking pots. Bedsheets. A ripped poster. Shirts and trousers. A beautiful dress. A smashed *chatty* pot. A teacup and half of a saucer.

Is this why Baba didn't come? Is it because there is so much to be done right here? So much to be cleaned up? Or is there some other, worse reason? Hasina feels a thickness rising in her throat.

But this is not what is worst of all. Worst of all is that in this, their once bustling street, there is now not a single sign of life.

No Aziza Begum, grower of fat, tasty *hodu hak*—her garden is black.

No sour old Rafee Hussain, spying on them—his house is a smoking patch of ash.

Sabikam Nahor's house stands, but in her garden is a mighty pair of buffalo horns, swarming with flies.

"Monu Mush!" Araf exclaims with a sob. "Why would they kill Monu Mush?" Hasina too feels like her heart will break. Big, beautiful Monu Mush. Why kill an animal? What has Monu Mush ever done to anybody? They walk on, Araf still sobbing.

Hasina's heart lurches as the brown speckled brick of their own house comes into view. Baba and Mama and Aunt Rukiah and Dadi, all of them could be inside their house, waiting. She walks a little faster, dragging on Araf's and Ghadiya's hands.

But something about her home seems stranger the closer she gets to it. Hasina cannot put her finger on what. All she knows is that the stone in her stomach is growing heavier. Why?

Right at that minute, Araf also sees the familiar brick of their house rising above the ruined trees. He drops her hand and starts to run. "Mama, Mama!" he calls out. "I am home!"

Araf, so predictable. Araf, so quick.

Suddenly, Hasina understands that stone-in-the-stomach feeling. Their house, like all the other houses on Third Mile Street, is still and silent. Maybe Mama and Baba aren't at home. Or maybe something far, far worse is waiting for them inside. She remembers the body she saw bobbing in the river and her gorge rises. "Araf! Wait!"

But he does not stop. Instead, she sees his little heels flying up even higher.

"Come on," Hasina shouts to Ghadiya, speeding after her little brother.

Araf jumps the old pots and pans in the road. He dips around the bits of metal roof and broken tree branches. He squeezes beneath what is left of their fence. Hasina pounds after him, but he is way ahead of her, already disappearing past the kitchen wall.

Hasina rounds the wooden wall of the kitchen and lets out a gasp. All that is left of it are the two walls. The cast-iron pots and pans, usually stacked neatly on a wire rack, are either crushed or have disappeared. The deep braziers that held the wood fires are all kicked over. The tidy bags of spices, twists of herbs, rattan boxes of tea, the tongs and spoons and chopping *suri* are all gone.

So is Araf. She can just see his heel as he kicks it up, running on past the kitchen toward the madrassa. Now he is calling, "Mama, Mama," and "Aunty, Aunty," expecting Aunt Rukiah to be in the madrassa. Hasina gives a final backward glance at their ruined kitchen and follows him.

Their madrassa, where she heard the helicopters for the first time, is only an outline of ash where the woven bamboo walls once stood. Gone are the wooden desks, their schoolbooks, their papers and pens. Hasina's precious math textbook with the kyat notes tucked in it, her savings toward the next math book, is gone. Only the blackboard where Aunt Rukiah showed them how to do their calculations is left. This stands out in the sunshine, all on its own. Araf is stopped here, staring, as if Aunt Rukiah has just written up a line of sums he doesn't understand.

"Araf, stop," Hasina calls out, slowing down, catching her breath, forcing her voice to be gentle. "Araf."

Araf glances back at her over his shoulder, but only briefly. "Baba, Baba!" he shouts. And then he is off again, dodging Hasina's arms as she tries to catch him. How is he able to run so fast? She herself is feeling light-headed, slow-limbed, the weight in her belly pulling her back.

"Araf! Stop!" she begs.

Araf races toward the wooden part of the house, where his bedroom is and where their parents sleep.

Warmth drains from Hasina's body.

She pelts after him. The closer she gets, the stronger the stink of smoke. Now, as she turns the corner, there is too much light. She looks up—Mama and Baba's bedroom is gone, her mother's scent of kohl and cloves, her father's piles of newspapers, the handsome clock that called the times for prayer. Araf's bedroom too, his toys and games and clothes. What is left of the wooden walls is charred and blackened.

She follows him through the doorway and inside. Araf races through the wooden building and into the brick heart of the house where Dadi Asmah and Aunt Rukiah sleep.

"Dadi," he bellows. "Dadi!" This is the only part of the house that is still intact. It reeks of smoke, but it looks and feels familiar.

Hasina catches up with him in their grandmother's room. Here are all Asmah's things. The shelf of books. The blue tin of biscuits. The frilly pink curtains. But the room is empty. Of their parents, their aunt, their grandmother, there is no sign at all in the house.

"Where *is* she?" Araf demands. He turns to Hasina, his face furious.

"Where are they? Where is everybody?"

CHAPTER 17

"Hello?"

Hasina startles at the voice. Is that Aunt Rukiah? With a thud of disappointment, she realizes it is only Ghadiya, calling out as she limps after them.

When Ghadiya arrives in Asmah's room her face is pale with shock. She glances quickly around, then hurries next door to her mother's room. When she comes back, her eyes are wide. "Isn't anybody here?"

"Nobody," Hasina replies.

"Where are they?" Araf demands, and then, "*Are they dead?*"

Here is the question Hasina has been asking herself since they first arrived at Third Mile Street. With each step through the house, she half-expected to come upon the twisted and blackened corpses of her family. Now at least she knows that her mother and father, grandmother and aunt escaped the fire that consumed half the house.

But did they escape only to die in some field like the

girl under the *longyi*? And if they aren't dead, have they run away and left them behind?

Suddenly, Hasina misses their hollow in the forest beneath the fringe of leaves, when she still had faith that Baba would come for them. Exhaustion washes through her. She half-climbs, half-falls onto her grandmother's bed.

Araf climbs across the bedspread to snuggle in beside her. Ghadiya burrows in on her other side. The three of them lie there, silent, for a long time.

Suddenly, Ghadiya sits bolt upright. "The hand phone!" she exclaims. "We are forgetting the hand phone."

She limps quickly to her mother's room, next door, Hasina and Araf following.

Aunt Rukiah kept her room tidy and, despite the fire, it remains as neat as she left it. The math textbook she brought with her from the south is propped up on the shelf beside her bed. There is little else in the room—or so Hasina thinks.

Ghadiya takes the chair from the dressing table and places it next to the curtains. Next, she climbs up onto the chair and, standing on tiptoe, reaches behind the curtain rod. Hasina gasps. Behind the curtain rod in the brick wall is some sort of hiding space. One that is totally undetectable from anywhere in the room.

Ghadiya plunges her hand into this space and pulls out a small, cloth-wrapped package. Inside is the cracked hand phone. "My mama would never leave Teknadaung without this," she exclaims triumphantly.

"Then where is she?"

Ghadiya's face falls, but Araf has a point. Finding the hand phone won't help them to work out where Baba, Mama, Dadi, and Aunt Rukiah are, or even if they're together. "I don't know." Her face suddenly brightens. "But we can call *my* baba!"

Just like Aunt Rukiah, she sweeps a finger along the glass surface and stabs at the screen. The phone makes a noise like a bird, then a high-pitched burst of sound. After that, like a miracle, Uncle Rashid's voice comes through the phone. "Hello?"

"Baba? It's Ghadiya!"

When Uncle Rashid hears Ghadiya's voice, he starts to sob. "You are alive!" Ghadiya, too, weeps. It is a few minutes before they can speak.

"Baba, Mama is not here."

"*What?*" Rashid's voice jolts out of the phone.

Ghadiya puts the phone on speaker and lays it on the bed so they can all hear.

"I don't know where Mama is. Or Uncle. Or Aunty. Or Dadi. Only Araf and Hasina are left here. We don't know what to do."

"Tell me exactly what happened." Rashid's voice is rough with emotion.

Ghadiya tells him about the attack. How it had come at night. About the men and the fires they lit.

"Sit Tat," her father grunts.

Ghadiya explains how they hid in the forest for five days. How they saw the Myanmar Army trucks leaving.

"They had to leave," Rashid says. "The Arakanese Army are attacking at the border."

Ghadiya continues, describing how the standpipe has been destroyed and most of Third Mile Street is now ash. "Baba, what should we do?"

"The television reports many attacks on Rohingya. Rohingya are being driven from their homes. Your mama, uncle, aunty, and dadi, all of them may have had to run."

Is that what happened? They *have* run? Without them? But where?

"Uncle, they have no permits," Hasina says.

Uncle Rashid's voice becomes even more serious. "Rohingya are not just being driven out of their homes, they are being driven out of Myanmar. They are allowed to leave, *if* they go to Bangladesh."

Hasina can feel the blood draining from her face. Bangladesh? That is *another country*.

"Last week, thousands of people arrived at the camps there in a single day." Uncle Rashid pauses. He takes a breath. "Hasina, listen to me carefully."

"Yes, Uncle Rashid."

"You are very brave. Ghadiya and Araf are lucky to have you take care of them. I thank you from the bottom of my heart."

Her uncle's praise brings the anguish of the past few days flooding back. Hasina has to swallow her tears.

"But Hasina, you will need to be braver still. Every Rohingya is now a target. You are in danger from the police, the Sit Tat, the Buddhist extremists. They all want you out. And if not out, then worse."

Hasina's blood runs cold.

"Our family is in your hands. You must keep everyone together in Teknadaung. Otherwise, we may never find you again. Can you do that?"

"I will try, Uncle."

"Good. I will do everything I can to find your parents, and your mama, Ghadiya. I will call when I have news."

Uncle Rashid goes on to explain that they must keep the phone hidden, that they must keep the battery charged. He gives them the number of a Rohingya lawyer in Sittwe, someone they can trust. Hasina only half-listens as Ghadiya writes it down. All she can think is, *Targets, we are targets. We are in danger.*

"I love you all." And Rashid rings off.

In the silence, Araf and Ghadiya look to Hasina, their eyes wide. How is she, a fourteen-year-old girl, meant to keep them safe from the police, the Sit Tat, the angry Arakanese, and Buddhists?

How will she keep her promise? And if she can't, what then?

CHAPTER 18

You are Rohingya. You are a target.

Her uncle's words wake Hasina early the next morning. She lets the others sleep on. She has thinking to do.

They may be targets, but they still have to eat and drink. And now, they must also make sure the hand phone is charged.

For this they will need to go to the family's stall at the bazaar. *Mama always charged the phone at the stall,* Ghadiya explained the night before. Hasina shivers— the last time she was there she came face to face with a Sit Tat soldier. Were they right in assuming that no trucks meant no more soldiers? If they are wrong, they could be walking into a trap of their own making.

On the other hand, there is an outside chance that the bazaar will have reopened and they will hear news of their family. A mist of hope films her eyes.

When the others wake, they all set off for the bazaar—they must stick together. They hide the phone and charger in a dented tiffin tin so they look to all the world like three children bringing lunch to their father. The last thing Hasina and Ghadiya do is leave their *numal*s on Rukiah's dressing table. Today, they will pass for Arakanese to strangers. As for those who know them? Their neighbors at the bazaar? Farmers in the paddy fields? People they've been passing in the street all of their lives? *We will just have to hope they don't turn us in,* Hasina thinks.

The morning is still cool as they walk along Third Mile Street. All over again, Hasina feels the painful shock of seeing a place once so familiar now so profoundly changed. They stop as they pass Monu Mush's horns.

"Goodbye, Monu Mush," Araf whispers, and slips his hand into Hasina's.

It may be dangerous to leave the house and walk to the bazaar, but at least the streets of Teknadaung will be familiar, normal. A bit of normal would be good.

When they reach Teknadaung, Hasina finds things here too have changed. The paddy fields around town are still empty of farmers. No Arakanese men sit around talking and spitting betel juice at the ground by the old Portuguese fort. Nobody is in at the International Aid office. Even the police station is quiet. Outside the Basic Education School is a sign: *Closed until farther notice.* The streets are empty of people apart from an Arakanese family packing up a cart to leave. They move like sleep-walkers, dazed, numb. *So it is not just Rohingya who have been affected by the violence,* Hasina thinks.

The bazaar entrance is also still—no women with

vegetables spread out on cloths, no muddle of motor-cycles and bicycles. The bazaar door, however, is open.

Hasina scans for soldiers. The coast is clear. Before they go in, she and Ghadiya take Araf aside. In a lowered voice, she tests him for the hundredth time.

"What language do we speak?" Hasina quizzes him.

"Myanmar language only."

"And the hand phone?" Ghadiya asks.

Araf puts a finger to his lips. "Tell no one. And the sign for *say nothing* is this," he whispers, blinking his eyes twice.

Hasina hugs her little brother, then waits for him to run ahead, as he normally does. Instead, he slips his hand into hers.

As they walk toward the shady bazaar, Hasina's heart starts beating faster. Just inside the entrance, she can see the same food stalls and teashops, vegetable stands and butchers that she has known forever. All of it so familiar, she can't help but scan for her father, head bent over a newspaper. Life continues. People still have to eat and sleep. People need news, people need each other. For this, Hasina is grateful.

But can Rohingya like her still be part of this com-munity?

One thing has changed. White bags are stacked in an enormous pile at the front of the bazaar, where the TV used to be. They are stamped with English letters that Hasina makes out as *A - I - D*. What does it mean? There's also a sign in Burmese script: *Cheap Rice*.

"Ah, Hasina! Araf!" calls a familiar voice.

Hasina startles as U Ko Yin appears beside her. She gives a small nod to Ghadiya, who melts away. Hasina bends her head to U Ko Yin in a respectful *shi-kho*.

"No veil today?" he asks, an unpleasant smirk on his face. "Greetings to your father in these … unusual times."

Hasina feels the stony weight of fear in her belly, and instinct tells her to be very careful here. Does U Ko Yin know something about her father? Is he giving her a message? Should she say that she doesn't know where he is? Can she lie? She catches Araf's eye; he blinks twice. Bless him.

"I have been wondering where your father is." U Ko Yin lowers his voice for effect. "Has he run away and left you?"

"He is attending to … family matters." It isn't entirely a lie. But it isn't entirely true either. She watches for U Ko Yin's response.

"I see," he grunts, fixing her with a hard stare, and Hasina feels her face heating up. "Well, I'm sure your father knows the rules. That a stall cannot stand un-attended for long. If you cannot do business, the bazaar will give your stall to someone who can. Those are the rules. I hope he's back open for business soon." U Ko Yin's voice turns lighter. "You know, I do need a place to sell my new line of foreigner foods—rice products, pulpy peanuts, very delicious." He gestures to the sacks of rice. "Medicines too." He shows her a pile of small boxes, full of shiny packets of pills.

He surveys his new venture with pride. Certainly, the

bags of rice and peanuts do look very smart, with their red and white packaging and the English letters stamped on them.

"Perhaps I can sell some of my things on your stall. Perhaps you and I can come to an arrangement?"

"I will pass on your request to my father," she replies.

U Ko Yin grins with his thick lips—a grin that does not reach his eyes.

"Or maybe, Araf, you would like to start working, a big strong boy like you. I can help you find a job. Your father would be pleased."

"A job in the bazaar?"

"Well, it would be in *a* bazaar," U Ko Yin responds.

"In your teashop?" Araf asks, confused.

"In *a* teashop." U Ko Yin's grin becomes a loud laugh that makes Hasina shiver. "Think it over."

"Thank you." She turns to go.

U Ko Yin grabs her by the arm then. His palm is clammy, his grip tight. Hasina gasps and her belly turns with revulsion. How dare he touch her! Every fiber of her being screams, *Let me go.* She forces herself to stay calm.

"Remember," he hisses, "come to *me* when you need help."

Hasina pulls herself free. She *shi-kho*s again and then, clasping Araf by the hand, hurries away, her belly still churning.

When they are out of sight of U Ko Yin, Ghadiya slips back beside Hasina. "Those bags of rice he is selling, I've seen that writing before," Ghadiya says. "They are from countries outside of Myanmar. Australia, Canada, Norway—countries that want to help our people. They are meant to be given to people in need, not sold."

Our people. The thought of people from outside of Rakhine wanting to help astonishes Hasina. Who might they be? Why would they want to help? It seems unlikely.

"Why would he be selling them if they should be free?" Hasina asks Ghadiya.

"Maybe because he wants one hundred percent profit."

"I might like to work in a teashop," says Araf to no one in particular.

"You would not, Araf," Ghadiya retorts sharply.

"I would be rich!"

"We don't need to be rich. We need to be safe. Besides, we have the family stall," Hasina says. She pictures those gleaming rows of boxes and tins, feels that nice full feeling. Is it true that the stall could be taken away?

Just then Ghadiya lets out a gasp. "Oh no!" Araf cries.

Up ahead is the Rohingya part of the bazaar. But today, there is no sound of Rohingya being spoken. No people at all. Just destruction. Stalls wrecked. Goods smashed. Hasina's stomach curls with anxiety. What will they find at their own stall?

Hasina moves quickly now, dragging Araf and Ghadiya behind her. None of them speaks until they are at the back of the bazaar, where their family stall should be.

The position is the only way Hasina recognizes their shop; everything else she sees is beyond her comprehension.

The roller door gapes open. The shelves are empty, swept clear of the goods for sale, which lie trampled on the floor. Sachets of shampoo have been slit open. Luxurious Danish biscuits have been tipped out of their tins and stamped to powder. *Dut* oozes from gashed tins. All of these beautiful, valuable, *useful* things—ruined. Now, there is nothing for her to count on.

Who could have done such a thing? She thinks of that young soldier outside the bazaar. Is this his work? Why not just steal? Why destroy like this so no one has the benefit of it? Why waste what is good?

For a long time, the three of them pick their way through the mess. They do not speak. What is there to say? Spilling rice on the floor is an offence to Allah. If her mother were here she would remind them that each grain must be picked with the fingers. But this is something worse than spilling.

Hasina feels like she's moving through mud. So much to cry over, she cannot cry at all. Ghadiya breaks the silence. "Remember, we came here to charge the phone."

Hasina pulls back the curtain to the alcove. What was the point? The electrical outlet was certain to be wrecked too.

Like the stall, the alcove is barely recognizable. One plastic chair remains but the clock is missing, as are the book of accounts and the strongbox with the money Baba was saving.

Ghadiya plugs the charger into the electrical outlet and connects the hand phone. It makes a little beep. "I don't get this. Everything else is destroyed, but not the outlet. See?"

Now it dawns on Hasina. The electrical outlet is part of the bazaar, so has not been wrecked. Only the boxes and packets of goods that belonged to her family have been destroyed. Like all the Rohingya stalls have been destroyed.

Suddenly it clicks. Someone wants to *make* them leave. Scare them so badly, they give up. And then, when they have given up, take their stall away according to the "rules," like U Ko Yin said.

Hasina feels a spike of rage and shame. Rage because she is sure she does not deserve this humiliation. And shame, because she would like to give up. Because she has let this happen and is powerless to stop it. Asmah says that shame leads to hate, which Hasina now knows to be true, because if she had that frightened soldier before her she does not know what she would be capable of doing. But the flare of rage doesn't last. In a moment it is gone and she feels emptier than before.

Beyond the curtain, there's a shout from Araf. She and Ghadiya rush out.

"Look at what I have found!" Araf is holding up a plastic toy soldier, perfectly intact. "And here's another. And another ..."

"This isn't wrecked either," Ghadiya says, pulling an intact tin of *dut* from the wreckage.

Together, they spend the rest of the morning picking up anything that isn't totally spoiled. Precious biscuits, some broken, some still in their stiff white paper collars. A strip of shampoo sachets that missed being slashed. Cans of coffee that are only dented. Handfuls of lentils that can still be eaten. Little by little, they rescue what they can, returning to the shelves what can be sold and setting aside what can still be used. They half-fill a bag with rice, a tin with broken biscuits, another with lentils. It takes hours, but finally, all that is left on the floor are a few sticky puddles.

Most important of all, the hand phone is charged and once more hidden in the tiffin tin.

Hasina bends to pick up the bundles of rubbish. "You two stay here," she instructs. "I will get rid of this."

As Hasina makes her way through the Rohingya part of the bazaar, it is the same story of pointless, wanton destruction. Empty stalls, the goods trampled. Equipment broken. Livelihoods destroyed. At the rubbish bin, she adds her pile of ruined things to the others. On her way back, she lingers outside the Brothers & Sons Puppet Stall.

Like all the other Muslim stalls, the Brothers & Sons Puppet Stall has been ransacked. Heads, legs, wings, arms are scattered across the floor. Strings knot upon themselves. Shredded costumes lie in pink and orange puddles. The platform where Amir used to sit is smashed. At the back of the shop, the roller door has been wedged half-open, hanging like a broken tooth before the dark storeroom. How long ago it seems that she stood here with Isak, watching Araf and Bashir tumbling with the kittens. How she yearns for that time. She was so happy then, although she hadn't known it. Happiness. Right now it seems impossible.

A tear spills down Hasina's cheek. She dashes it away, but another follows. She's too tired now for rage and shame. All she feels is defeat, a sadness too big for her body. She wills herself not to cry.

Just then, a gray-white streak flashes across the floor to her feet. A pair of deep blue feline eyes stares up at her.

"Daamini!" Hasina cries. The cat meows back. Hasina scoops her up and holds her close, burying her face in soft fur. "Daamini, Daamini," she murmurs over and over again.

The pretty little cat's coat is rough in patches. She's scrawny and one of her ears is gashed and bent. But she is alive.

Isak and Daamini. They were inseparable. Where is Isak now? And the other stallholders in the market? Where are her neighbors? Where are Tara and Rosie and Aman? Where are the children she played with and fought with?

Deep inside herself she guesses at the answer, and the tears come, hot and thick. They sting her face, and she wipes them against Daamini's fur.

She and Isak. Back on that day with the kittens, she felt like life was just about to unfold for both of them.

She felt protected. All this has been taken from them by those men with eyes like demons. By the soldiers in their trucks. By the police who beat the men and women left behind.

She must have let her feelings get the better of her and started to squeeze the poor cat, because all of a sudden Daamini gives a sharp meow and leaps out of Hasina's arms.

"Daamini," Hasina pleads. "Sorry! Come back. Please!"

But Daamini is already streaking across the platform of the Brothers & Sons Puppet Stall. The little tabby pauses briefly beneath the roller door before dashing into the darkness beyond. Hasina feels a terrible pang of regret. This cat, Isak's cat, came to her and now she has chased her away.

"Daamini!" she calls, crawling across the platform toward the roller door. She bends down to peer inside the dark storeroom. It smells of cotton and glue. "Here, puss."

Not even a meow or flash of a tail.

Hasina sits back on her haunches. Now that she's found Daamini, she cannot bear to let her go. But the cat is deep in the storeroom. She will have to go in after her, into the dark.

She bends her head beneath the roller door once more. "Here, pussy-kitten," she calls.

A faint meow echoes from beyond the storeroom door. Relief floods Hasina's heart. "Daamini!"

But the cat does not answer this time. With a deep

breath, Hasina drops flat and squeezes under the steel door. Light knifes past her into the gloom. Dozens of painted eyes stare back at her, and Hasina shudders. But slowly, as her own eyes become accustomed to the dark, she relaxes. It looks like the soldiers didn't come in here.

"Here, puss. Here, Daamini."

Another faint meow. She wriggles farther until she is all the way into the storeroom. She eases herself up into a crouch. Darkness crowds around her.

"Where are you, Daamini?"

This time, instead of an answering meow, a groan splits the darkness—or is it a growl?

Hasina freezes. Her heart pounds so hard it's the only thing she can hear. All she can think of are Uncle Rashid's words. *You are a Rohingya, you are a target.*

Stupid, stupid, stupid. How could she be so stupid? Days and days hiding in the forest, only to walk into this trap!

Another groan rends the air. But this time, there is something pathetic about that groaning voice. Something that pulls her closer.

She forces herself to take a deep, slow breath in and ignores the hammering in her chest.

"*Mingalar bar?*"

Silence.

"Hello?" she tries in Arakanese.

Still silence. Now her heart is pounding again. She takes a step deeper in.

"*Aasso-lamu alaikum,*" she calls out softly.

Back comes the reply, softer still. "*Wa alaikum aasso-lam.*"

Each syllable is forced out, drenched in pain. But she knows that this groaning person is also Rohingya. Not only that, the voice … it is familiar.

"Uncle Amir?" she calls out. "Uncle Sultan? … Isak?"

"*Wa alaikum aasso-lam,*" the voice whispers.

Isak. It is *Isak*.

Now Hasina's heart is pounding with excitement. "Where are you?"

Another groan comes from the back corner of the room. "Who's there?" The words are like rubble in his mouth.

"It is me, Hasina."

Isak lays hidden behind a box full of old plastic sheeting. He holds his head up into the shaft of light. The boy with the tight curls and dazzling smile is not as she remembers him. His eyes are almost swollen shut, his mouth and nose crusted in blood. His voice trembles with the effort of speaking. "Hasina? Be careful. The men, the soldiers, they are out there …"

Hasina kneels next to him. If only she had some water to give him. "Isak, the men have gone. Can you sit up?"

With a grunt, he pushes one arm against the cement and raises himself partway off the floor. He pants, then pushes once more. Now at least he is sitting up.

"I am going to help you to get out of here," Hasina tells him. She takes his arm to support him, and they half-crawl, half-walk to the doorway.

Isak flinches as they emerge into daylight. His

shirt and *longyi*, his face, and his hair are crusted with blood. His right shoulder droops. He cannot put his full weight on his left side. Blood oozes thickly through his shirt.

Hasina searches through the debris on the floor for a cloth. She finds one, torn and trampled. This she opens out and wraps around Isak's shoulders. She looks around. The market is still empty.

"I am going to take you to our stall."

"Daamini," he croaks. The blue-eyed tabby appears, quiet as smoke. Hasina scoops her up and the three of them start to move.

Slowly, slowly, step by painful step, Isak limps forward, his body heavy against Hasina's. He keeps his head down so that if someone passes, they won't see his injuries. They both know those injuries mark him out as Rohingya.

By the time they reach Hasina's stall, Isak is clammy and pale. Hasina brings him through the curtain to the alcove behind.

Ghadiya and Araf are waiting for her, their faces full of worry.

"Where have you been—" Ghadiya begins, then sees Isak.

"Isak!" Araf cries out. "What happened?"

"Water, please."

Hasina rushes to fill a cup from the bazaar *chatty* pot. When she returns, Isak is sitting on the remaining plastic chair. He drinks thirstily while Hasina tears a strip from his *longyi* and wets it. Gently, she cleans the blood from his face, his hands, and the gash in his side, while Isak tells his story.

"Men attacked our house at night. They burnt it down. My father, Uncle Sultan, Bashir, we escaped to the bazaar. Other Rohingya were here too. Others hid in the forest. Many ran away.

"My father, my uncle, Bashir, we all hid here. For two days, we lived in the stall, behind the roller door. But then soldiers—Sit Tat—came. Their leader ordered the soldiers to round everyone up. Then they took away anyone who looked Rohingya. Anyone with dark skin."

Round them up. With a jolt, Hasina recognizes those words. Was that the day she was outside the bazaar? The day she encountered the young soldier?

"They were looking for ARSA fighters. They took us and Bashir, my uncle, out the back. They lined us up and asked us questions." Isak pauses, gathers his breath. "They beat us. They cut us. They left us for dead. Only, I wasn't dead. I crawled back into the bazaar. In the morning they came for the bodies with trucks. I could hear them shouting about loading the stiffs. I have been in the storeroom ever since."

"But what about Bashy?" Araf cries. "Where is Bashy?"

Isak turns away. When he faces them again, his eyes are full of tears. He looks broken, like one of his puppets. "I am the only Brother and Son now," he says softly.

Hasina's head spins. Isak is no ARSA fighter. He is a boy. And Bashir was a small child.

There's a soft meow, and Daamini rubs against Isak's

legs. Araf picks her up and puts her in his lap. Daamini sits, purring.

"Isak, did you hear anything about our parents? They've disappeared too."

"I heard the soldiers talking. They are pushing people to Bangladesh. Many people from this town went there. Hasina, I heard someone say they saw your father."

Relief floods through her. Baba!

"Was anyone with him?" Ghadiya asks anxiously.

"Yes. Your mother, Ghadiya, and yours too, Hasina."

Mama and Aunt Rukiah were with Baba. If only she could be certain it were true. But that also means Asmah is still missing. Hasina is torn. Who should she hope has survived?

There is another question. What can they do with Isak? Should they take him back to what remains of their home? Will he be offended if she asks? It is not proper for her to have a boy, even Isak, in her house. But these are strange times. Proper doesn't seem to count anymore.

Araf solves the problem for her. "Isak, come to our house. We will take care of you."

Isak lifts his broken mouth into a stiff smile. "Maybe tomorrow, Araf. I don't think I can walk there. Right now, all I want to do is sleep."

"Tomorrow you will come," Araf insists.

Hasina sighs. If only she could feel so sure about what tomorrow would bring.

CHAPTER 19

They settle Isak back into the storeroom. Araf brings him water to drink. Ghadiya opens a dented tin of *dut* for him. They promise to return in the morning.

All the way home, Hasina thinks about Isak. How alone he must feel, the only brother, the only son. At least she has Araf and Ghadiya. And there was news of Baba, Mama, and Aunt Rukiah. Even her house is still partly standing.

Isak's news brings fresh questions; has Baba left for Bangladesh without them? Hasina cannot believe this is possible.

When they arrive home, something is not right. Someone has dumped a pile of rags in front of their house.

As Hasina draws closer, she sees it is not rags, but a person.

And then the rags move, as if whipped up by the wind, and take a human form. A small person stands upright. With a jolt, Hasina recognizes who that person is.

"Dadi Asmah!"

In a few bounds, Hasina is beside her grandmother. "You're here!"

She is about to wrap Asmah in the biggest of hugs when she stops short at the sight of her grandmother up close. Dadi Asmah looks like she might crumple under a big hug. Her eyes are red-rimmed and sunken. Her shoulder bows, her head moves slowly and stiffly on her neck. The hawk-like nose, so familiar on her face, is now sharper, bonier, as if it is stretching the skin around her eyes and hollow cheeks.

"Hasina!" Dadi Asmah's voice is a croak so dismal that Hasina barely recognizes her own name. What has happened to the voice that told so many stories? Then her grandmother smiles.

That smile! It is the same as ever, and what it shows right now is the deepest joy. And those red eyes shine with tears that run down Dadi Asmah's dusty skin, leaving wet tracks.

She croaks again. "Araf! Ghadiya!"

From behind her, Hasina hears Araf and Ghadiya's shouts of "Dadi, Dadi!" She feels rather than hears Araf's footsteps as he accelerates, about to launch himself into Asmah's arms.

Hasina is just turning, just about to stop him, when a fierce creature leaps out from behind Dadi Asmah's legs and plants itself between Asmah and Araf. Dark eyes glower from beneath a ragged fringe as the creature growls and hisses a warning through bared teeth. The message is clear: *Leave her alone, or you will have me to deal with.*

Araf is so stunned that he changes direction midair and lands behind Hasina, clamping himself to her leg. Ghadiya too pulls in beside Hasina, but instead of hiding, Hasina senses that Ghadiya is there to help her withstand this new threat—this spitting, growling, fierce creature that has come between them and their grand-mother.

It takes Hasina a moment to realize that it is a girl. A brown, cat-eyed, long-nailed, tangle-haired, absolutely filthy little scrap of a girl.

"Hush, hush," Dadi Asmah soothes the fierce girl, placing a hand on her shoulder. The girl stops growling, but she does not relax that fighting stance.

Now Hasina can see that she is tiny. Hardly a threat at all, unless fierceness alone counts. Like Asmah, the girl looks weak and exhausted. When was the last time these two ate?

"Ghadiya," she asks her cousin in a soft voice, so as not to set the cat girl off into another round of hissing and growling, "those biscuits, please?"

Ghadiya hands her the tin of broken biscuits. Slowly, gently, Hasina removes the lid and extends the tin toward the girl. "Would you like one? Go on."

The girl glances at Dadi Asmah, who nods her permission. The girl cautiously extends her fingers, then, quick as a flash, snatches a biscuit from the tin. Never taking her gaze from Hasina, she licks the biscuit.

Then nibbles at it, then crunches it, then crams the rest into her mouth, chewing hungrily. The biscuit is gone in a heartbeat.

Hasina offers her the whole biscuit tin and the girl takes it in her hands as if it is something precious. With a *shi-kho*, she hands it to Asmah. Asmah offers her the tin in turn, and once again the girl takes a biscuit, this time crunching into it noisily.

Meanwhile, Dadi Asmah hugs her grandchildren. Araf first, Ghadiya next, and finally, Hasina. Nothing feels so good as being wrapped in her grandmother's arms. *At last*, Hasina thinks, *we really are home.*

They retreat beneath the brick veranda, the girl and Asmah passing the tin of biscuits between them, while Hasina lights a fire, boils water, makes tea, hands her grandmother a cracked cup. Asmah takes a sip; a smile of pleasure warms her face.

"Dadi," says Araf, his voice serious, "we do not know where Mama or Baba are. Or Aunt Rukiah. We do not know where everyone is."

Asmah's smile fades. She seems to shrivel before their eyes.

"I left your parents a few days ago." Parents! That meant Baba and Mama and Aunt Rukiah were alive. Hasina's heart leaps with relief. And yet Dadi Asmah's face is so sad. "They have gone from Teknadaung. They are walking to Bangladesh."

So, what Isak had heard was true. But that meant …

"Bangladesh! You mean they left us behind?"

Asmah places her cup of tea on the ground. She

hangs her head. "Yes, they left you behind. *We* left you behind."

Hasina feels a vice-like grip squeezing her heart. Tears scald her eyes and constrict her throat. She turns her face away from her grandmother's. She cannot believe this is true. Ever since they'd run to the High Forest she'd wondered why Baba had not come for them. Now she wonders, *Did he even look for us?*

Asmah gives a deep sigh and continues her story. "On the night the men came … it felt like the end of the world. We were like animals. We were so afraid." She shivers at the memory of it. "Baba saw you three run up the road. And then, he saw men come from that direction. Bad men with covered faces. And fire."

Hasina remembers the three men waiting by the standpipe. The man in the middle had lit first one torch and then the other. With those torches, those men destroyed her home. The realization hits her like a blow.

"Your baba was already out of the house. He was going to find you. But …"

Tears well up in Asmah's eyes, they leave shiny tracks along her cheeks.

"… everywhere was on fire. We ran outside. There was screaming, crying. Our neighbors and our friends. Some ran to the river, others ran to the paddy fields."

Asmah wipes away her tears. "We ran to the Lower Forest. We were not alone. There were others from Eight Quarters. All night we watched our homes burn."

Hasina's heart hurts at the thought of her grandmother watching the home her father built burning.

"Before the dawn, the men who had set Eight Quarters on fire came to the forest. When they found us, they told us that they would let us live if we left. If we went back to where we came from."

"Back to where we came from? But this is where we come from." Araf's voice is tiny, confused, tearful. "This is where we all come from."

Asmah continues. "At first, it was just us, from Eight Quarters. Then, as we walked it was others from Teknadaung. Then from other villages and towns. Sometimes the men came back, to make sure we kept going and did not turn for home."

Hasina thinks of the young soldier's officer barking, *Round them up*. What if such a man found you, all alone in the woods? If it was her, would she have run too? Would she have left Araf and Ghadiya and saved herself?

"But where are they going?" Araf demands.

"To the Naf River. From there they can cross into Bangladesh. There are camps there. Camps where our people are gathering in great numbers."

"But why didn't they wait for *us*?" Araf's voice trembles.

"They were being forced to go, Araf," Ghadiya explains, her voice dull. "They had no choice."

So this is how Ghadiya has felt all along, Hasina thinks. Empty. Angry. Like the world has lost its color.

Ghadiya breaks the silence with a question.

"Why didn't you go with them, Dadi?"

"I did. But I cannot walk fast. I got lost. I too was left behind." Asmah smiles bitterly.

"I didn't mind. I thought, if I have to die, then let it be in my home."

Hasina shudders. Is that what will happen now? They will all die here. And her parents will never know it.

"How long until they walk there?" Araf asks.

"I don't know."

"How will we know when they are there?"

"I don't know," Asmah repeats. Her skin pales and she leans against the brick wall, closing her eyes. In the late afternoon sun, Hasina can almost see the bones beneath her grandmother's skin. How long was she without food? Without water? Does she need medicine? Or just sleep?

Ghadiya breaks the silence. "How did you find the girl?"

"The girl" looks up, as if she knows that she is being talked about.

"She is a Mro girl. And she understands Burmese." Asmah demonstrates. "Can you find me a flower?" she asks the girl, who nods and runs off immediately. While she is gone, Dadi Asmah tells her story.

"When I lost the others, I followed a stream back to the river, then followed the river. Our own Farak River, which I know so well. I slept beneath a tree one night, in a cave on another. On the third day, I found this girl.

"I was walking upstream. There is a place where the river opened out, and the forest sloped upward—a good place to stop and take a drink. This is where she was.

She was among her family, trying to wake them up, but they were all dead. They are not Muslim. They are not Buddhist. They were people of the forest."

Hasina glances toward the cat girl, searching the ashen gardens for green shoots. How it must have hurt to leave those sleeping bodies behind. How hard it is to be the one who is left alive.

"Was it Sit Tat?" Araf demands. Hasina stares at him in surprise. How quickly he has learned these words. Again, she wonders how much of this he understands.

Asmah shakes her head. "So many people have been killed. Some by Sit Tat, who fight for a Buddhist nation. Others by the Arakanese Army, who fight for an Arakanese nation. But this girl's family were killed by ARSA, who fight for the Rohingya. Our people killed her people."

Hasina reels. This girl's family had been killed in her name, as a Rohingya. What say did she, Hasina, have in this act? None at all.

The Mro girl returns, a purple orchid in her fingers. She holds it as if it is a precious jewel. She is about to hand it to Asmah, but then she turns and gives it instead to Hasina.

Hasina holds the flower flat in her hand. It looks like a miracle. But what good are miracles if she cannot save those she loves? She places the flower on the ground.

She stands up. "Araf, time to let Dadi rest. And this girl too."

Mechanically, Hasina looks at the sky. Maghirb, the dusk prayer—time to cook dinner. She realizes this is the first time she has remembered prayers since the attack.

And what, she asks herself, is the point of praying? What is the point of a god?

She turns automatically toward the makeshift kitchen, pours the rice and lentils salvaged from the bazaar into a *deshi*. Lights a fire.

The perfume of cooking rice fills the air, but she gets no pleasure from it.

She spoons the meal onto a tray, places it in front of her grandmother and the girl, her brother and cousin. This is an act of love. But she does not feel love, only numbness.

She sits to eat. "*Bismillah karo hamam rahin,*" she murmurs. She fills her mouth with grains of rice. But she might as well be eating the ash from the houses burnt around her.

We are targets, she thinks. *Nobody wants us*, she thinks.

But they did want each other, her family. Or so she had believed.

Her baba had made her promise to keep the three of them together so that he could find them. But that same baba has left them behind. Like Monu Mush's horns in the ash. Like the broken puppets at the Brothers & Sons Puppet Stall.

There is nothing left to rely on.

Hasina, the girl she once was, who loved geometry, who could take a shot on goal from the midfield, who could speak Myanmar and English and loved her baba above all, that girl is gone. As dead and lifeless as Rivka, the girl in the field covered only by a *longyi*. In her place is the Hasina she is now: a shell that once was that girl. A body with a head, with hands, with a belly. But empty, because her heart is now broken and she fears it will never mend.

CHAPTER 20

The monsoon settles over Rakhine. Rain swells the Farak River and washes the ash away. It leaks through the roof at Third Mile Street, drip, drip, dripping into a corner of Aunt Rukiah's room. The sound wakes Hasina long before Fagr. She lies there waiting to see if the sun will rise, Ghadiya on one side, Araf on the other. When the dawn does finally come, all she feels is sad; the time when her family was there and she was whole slips farther away.

She rouses Ghadiya and Araf before padding into Dadi Asmah's room to wake Cat Girl. They gather all the buckets and tins they possess and walk for half an hour to a flat place by the river. Sometimes, out in the center in the fast water, a body drifts past. One time, Hasina sees five footballs bobbing in the current. Too late, she realizes that these balls have hair, noses, and mouths.

Back home, after prayers, Hasina sends the children out to forage. Cat Girl is excellent at finding food. She has also taken a shine to Araf. There is nowhere he can go where she will not follow. Each morning, she takes him by the hand and they return with wild guavas, or wild garlic. Occasionally an egg. But it is never enough for all of them. One breakfast, Cat Girl presents him with a juicy white grub. "Yeuch," he says. But hunger wins. "Tastes like chicken."

Ghadiya lights the fire for cooking while Hasina measures how much of their rice, salvaged from the stall, remains. At first, the grains go all the way up to her elbow. Then to her forearm. Then only to her wrist. Each day, breakfast gets a little smaller. And she learns that hunger burns in the belly just like fear.

They eat off the communal tray on the veranda. If Dadi Asmah is feeling poorly, as she often is, Cat Girl or Araf takes her a small tin lid of rice. Dadi Asmah does not eat all of hers. Instead, she gives it to Araf or Cat Girl; she thinks Hasina doesn't know.

Then it is time for the bazaar. Hasina rubs *thanaka* onto her face, as she used to when taking lunch to Baba. But this is *thanaka* from Aunt Rukiah's dressing table. Her own jar, along with everything else that was once hers, is now ash. Only her *numal* remains, and that she leaves folded on her aunt's dressing table, next to Ghadiya's. The square of orange and purple cloth is a bright reminder of how things used to be.

A few days after Dadi Asmah comes home, Eid al-Adha, the festival of the sacrifice, begins. "Last year, we had fireworks," Araf reminds Hasina as she puts him to bed.

"I remember," she sighs. Tara had brought pencils

to the madrassa as presents. Aziza gave her mother a *hodu hak*. Now, there are no other Rohingya to exchange gifts with. Only the old and injured are left. How they survive, she cannot imagine.

Even the Arakanese have been leaving in droves. Teknadaung feels empty, as if time itself has stopped.

Yet, the days pass. A whole week goes by. Then another.

The bazaar is still quiet and the Rohingya section, deserted. The army may be gone, but her Arakanese neighbors and their old customers are either too scared or too ashamed to come near them. Only the very poor and penny-pinchers venture to the back of the market.

"I'll give you fifty kyats," a woman barks, holding up a packet of shampoo worth two hundred. Hasina has no choice but to take it. How else will she pay for the food they need?

"It is not against the law to *be* a Rohingya," Isak proclaims, pretending defiance. He is right. But that doesn't mean it is safe. That is why the two of them stick together when she is at the bazaar. Why she often brings Ghadiya or Araf with her. Her uncle's reminder— *stay together*. His words—*you are a Rohingya, you are a target*—still ring in her ears.

Isak is slowly rebuilding the Brothers & Sons Puppet Stall. Hasina knows it is because he needs something to do with his hands. Nowadays, he is accompanied by princes, magicians, or *nagar*s as well as Daamini. The gray and white cat loves to prowl through the alcove, emitting high-pitched yowls when she finds something to her taste. Isak brings news too. "The school has not yet reopened," he tells her. "Nobody thinks it ever will." And later, "The farmers are still not in their paddy fields. They should be fertilizing by now. There will be a rice shortage for sure."

Hasina doesn't know how he lives when she doesn't see him. His eyes are too dark now. At times, he curls deep into himself and far away from her, closer to the dead than the living.

"When are you coming to live with us?" Araf demands. "Dadi Asmah has given permission."

But Isak refuses. "It would not be proper," he says. "Besides," he confides in Hasina, "you have enough to do." She wonders if he feels closer to his father and uncle and brother here in the bazaar. If only she could tell him that *she* needs him. That she aches to have him around, not just to remind her of how life used to be either.

Her other regular companion is U Ko Yin, his questions as relentless as the rain. He waits until Isak has gone and then pounces.

"Where is your baba? Has he run away?"

"You have so few things to sell on your stall. How will you survive?"

"Why doesn't Araf come work for me?"

"He should mind his own business," Isak storms. "Nobody here likes U Ko Yin. Haven't you noticed that nobody is buying his foreigners' rice?"

That may be, but still, U Ko Yin's questions make her worry. How will they survive? She doesn't know.

It is on a particularly dull, wet day that U Ko Yin

drops by to spy on Hasina just as Isak is testing out his new ogre puppet.

"Oh dear," begins U Ko Yin, "I see your father is *still* not here."

"No," growls Isak, "but *I* am here. And so is my friend." Then Isak pulls the ogre's string so that he rises magically into the air, his mouth opening to show rows of scary, sharp teeth. Right then, Daamini emits one of her chilling yowls.

"Urk," gulps U Ko Yin, startled by the snapping mouth and realiztic fangs. "Ah well, must be going."

When he is out of sight, Isak and Hasina laugh and laugh—and then stop.

"When was the last time you laughed?" Isak asks Hasina.

"I don't know," she admits. Isak's eyes darken, his face falls.

"Me neither. My uncle Sultan used to say, *Laugh too hard and you will have to cry*."

If only she could cry. If only she could feel again. But Hasina's heart is too broken for feeling.

One day at the rubbish pile she hears a sharp *mwwouch*, a sound between a kiss and a whistle. It is the kind Arakanese man who changed the channel on the TV a whole year ago, the day the helicopters came.

The man is busily breaking up boxes for the rubbish. He seems so engrossed in his tasks that, for a moment, Hasina thinks she's misheard. But then, again, there's that smooching sound. She turns. He catches her eye and nods, almost without seeming to nod.

Hasina feels a prickle of fear along the back of her neck. She is about to scurry away when he walks close, as if to pass her. Under his breath he mutters, "You have not run away, like the others."

"No," she replies. To anybody watching, it would look as if the man isn't speaking to her at all.

"You are not safe. We cannot control our own people and the military wish to destroy yours."

His words bring back that old stone-in-her-stomach feeling.

"Bad men are coming in on trucks. Kidnapping girls. Stealing young boys. If you must stay, be careful."

Then the man turns and leaves the rubbish mound. Where he was standing is a white bag. Hasina picks it up. It is full of rice.

That night, while Dadi Asmah is still awake, Hasina tells her about the Arakanese man's warning.

"Maybe Araf and Ghadiya should stay here with you?" Hasina frets. Then, all of the things worrying her seem to flow out of her. "And the rice he gave us will only last us so long. And we are running out of things to sell at the stall. We need to harvest our paddy field. But how we will manage it, Dadi?"

"We will find a way," says Dadi Asmah, her eyes already heavy, ready for sleep. She reminds Hasina of the teachings of the Qur'an. "No pain, big or small, is wasted or meaningless. All pain is counted and compensated by Allah."

Pain, Hasina thinks, *is something I have in abundance.* There is the pain of being abandoned, of losing almost everything, of having to carry on despite it all. "Maybe we should have run away, like Baba and Mama," Hasina growls.

Dadi Asmah sighs sadly. She puts an arm around Hasina and pulls her close.

"Hasina, it takes strength to stay. Courage too. We will find a way."

The next day at the bazaar, Hasina complains to Isak. "When Dadi Asmah says *we*, she means *me*."

"I have no *we*," Isak murmurs. "I have just me."

A tailor opens his stall again in the Rohingya section. A few more customers venture to the back of the bazaar. And then, before Hasina knows it, one month has become two.

◈◈

It is as the rains are at their thickest that fever breaks out in Teknadaung. Dadi Asmah develops a nasty cough that racks her tiny frame. A new fear squeezes Hasina's chest. What would she do without Dadi?

U Ko Yin adds white boxes of fever medicine, foreigners' pills, and many people come to buy them. They even start to buy his foreigners' rice. Finally he's selling something. Every few days, a man in a brown *longyi* tops up the boxes of medicines and the bags of rice with *AID* stamped on them.

"That rice will sell too," U Ko Yin boasts to Hasina. "So many people have left that there will be no harvest.

All those paddy fields will spoil. The grains will go yellow and then fall. And when that happens"—U Ko Yin rubs his hands with glee—"then even foreigners' rice will be worth a fortune."

Soon, Hasina is facing her own rice shortage. One morning, there is only rice to her knuckles in the bag the Arakanese man gave her. She goes to Dadi Asmah's bedroom. She runs her fingers along the rows of books. *How much would they fetch?* she wonders with a pang. What about Aunt Rukiah's math book? Is there anything else here they can sell if they have to?

Dadi Asmah finds her fingering her books. She asks for an explanation.

"I have too many mouths to feed. We need to sell things," Hasina retorts sharply.

Hasina knows it is clear to her grandmother that she means Cat Girl, who eats like a bird and brings food through foraging. Hasina knows she is not being fair.

"One house, many rooms, room for all. That is our Burma. Otherwise we would be as bad as the men with eyes like demons," her grandmother reminds her. "You will find a way, Hasina."

And then her grandmother coughs so hard, Hasina fears she will break into pieces. Later that day, when U Ko Yin comes by to ask his daily questions, Hasina wonders how much those medicines with the red letters stamped on them cost. Is it true that they are meant to be free? That they are meant to help people like her? She would like some help.

I must find a way, she thinks.

If there is a bright spot, it is Rashid's calls on the hand phone. She is familiar now with its metallic chirrup. She has even run her fingers across the keypad, worked out how to use the buttons. At the end of each call, Rashid asks them all to recite the number of the lawyer in Sittwe. The man who can help. "Call him if you need him."

But the lawyer is far away in Sittwe, the big city. He cannot find them food.

Late one afternoon, Isak rushes over, his face alight.

"Hanif the tailor has heard people from Teknadaung are at a camp called Kutupalong. Ask your uncle. Maybe he can find out if it is true."

When Uncle Rashid calls back a few nights later, his voice is animated. "Tara's mother, Sabikam Nahor, is in the camp. She thinks she saw Aunt Rukiah." Then he calls again. "Sabikam Nahor says someone else has reported seeing two women and a man from Third Mile Street. It could be them."

The news leaves Hasina full of hope that soon her parents will be found and maybe even return. That they will take care of things as they once did. But hope also hurts. In the night, all that hope drips away. She turns to Ghadiya, sleeping beside her, and whispers, "Soon we will have no more rice ... We need to harvest, but how will we do that?" The only reply is Ghadiya's breathing.

So Hasina gets up before Fagr. She wakes the others. She leads them to the bank of the river, where they collect water. She sits behind the dwindling goods at the stall. She comes home with their shopping.

She lights the evening fire. She makes plans with Asmah and Ghadiya.

Two months become almost three. The rain begins to ease. The days cool down. The paddy plants begin to droop, heavy with rice grains. In the mornings, fog rises from the river.

But through it all, the hollow feeling remains. For now it is months since the world as she knew it was burnt to ash. Nothing can ever be the same again.

CHAPTER 21

It is on a crisp, fresh morning that the trucks return
to town.

They are on their way to their paddy field—Dadi
Asmah, Ghadiya, Araf and Cat Girl as well. Harvest time
is coming, and nobody has checked the rice crop for
pests, or checked the rice heads.

Hasina's heart jumps when she first sees the trucks.
The day at the bazaar flashes through her mind—the
young soldier, the terrifying voice.

"Hide!" she hisses to the others, as she drags Araf
toward an oleander bush.

Only Ghadiya stands her ground. She points out that
these are not the olive-green or brown Sit Tat trucks.
They do not have long rows of facing bench seats for
soldiers to sit. These are trucks of all different sorts.
Some have shiny new materials piled up on flat beds
behind the cab. Some are dump trucks with massive
tippers on the back, full of gray gravel. Others are cargo
trucks, carrying woven bamboo sheets, aluminum posts,

rolls and rolls of thick blue plastic sheeting, and rolls and rolls of wire. One massive truck is carrying two yellow bulldozers chained to the deck.

"What are they here for, Dadi?" Hasina asks.

"Nothing good," Dadi Asmah replies, and walks on ahead, leaning on Ghadiya.

It is impossible not to feel impressed at the arrival of so many shiny trucks, with their big wheels and brightly painted sides. Araf, hand in hand with Cat Girl, lingers, gazing at them all. "I do like trucks," he sighs longingly.

"Come on, we'd better catch up with Dadi." But Araf won't budge. He's enthralled by the trucks. Cat Girl waits patiently by his side.

The trucks are lined up past the open field where Hasina once played soccer, at the edge of Eight Quarters District. Only a few months ago, this was a busy place, full of houses and kids and animals and gardens, separated from the flooded paddy fields by an empty spit of land. Now, gray ash marks where those houses and families were, and it is the spit of land that is busy with people.

For along with the trucks and their drivers come construction workers, men wearing hard hats. Truck drivers sleep in the big cabins of their vehicles—Hasina sees them emerging with sleep-filled eyes, yawning and stretching and adjusting their *longyi*s. These men in hard hats are building themselves a village. They are unloading woven bamboo mats, setting up sleeping huts, running a hose down to the river.

How long are these people planning to stay? What are they here for? Hasina hopes that Dadi is wrong, and that they are here to help those who left when they return. With a pang, she thinks of her parents and her aunt. She can't wait for the day when they come home. If only there was some more news of them.

Hasina's thoughts are interrupted by Araf tugging on her hand. He's pointing to a red truck with a blue peacock and the words *Sittwe Transport* painted on the side. A man, the driver, with rumpled black hair and ears that stick out, has just tumbled out of the cab. Not only is the truck memorable, but so is the brown *longyi* he is wearing. It is crumpled at the hem, which shows he doesn't care if he ties it at the top or at the bottom.

This is what Hasina notices about him, anyway. Araf notices the truck. While Cat Girl notices Araf noticing the truck.

"Cool," says Araf. "Whoa. I would like to drive a truck like that man. I would drive in the morning to my teashop. At lunch, I would work in a teashop. We would be rich."

At the sound of Araf's voice, the man looks up. "So you like my truck, do you?"

Hasina stares at the man in astonishment. Few Burmese or even Arakanese know how to speak the Rohingya language. Araf drops Hasina's hand and takes a step closer to Brown *Longyi*. The man continues, "You would make a very good teashop boy." Then he grins, exposing teeth red with betel nut.

Hasina moves closer to Araf on one side, Cat Girl on the other.

"Hey, what is your name?" asks the truck driver.

"Araf. What is your name?"

The man laughs at Araf's cheekiness. "Zaw Gyi." He turns back to his truck and opens the cab door. "Would you like to see inside, Araf?"

"Yes, please!" Araf scrambles up the steps.

With a lurch of fear, Hasina remembers the warning of the kind Arakanese. She remembers her mother's stories too, about the boys taken to work as teashop slaves, though Hasina never believed them. Were the stories true? Is this the sort of man who kidnaps boys like Araf? Araf is already scrambling up into the cabin. How easy it would be for Zaw Gyi to just drive away.

Cat Girl doesn't seem to like Zaw Gyi either. Or maybe she doesn't like to see Araf out of her reach. She leaps forward and grips Araf's leg, refusing to let him climb in any farther.

Zaw Gyi laughs. Cat Girl emits a low growl.

"Woah!" exclaims Zaw Gyi, taking a step back. "Maybe you'd better come back later, Araf. Alone."

"Humph," Araf protests.

Even Hasina can't help but smile. "Come out of the truck, Araf. Dadi is waiting."

Dadi Asmah and Ghadiya are far ahead now, already at the edge of the construction village.

Araf climbs down reluctantly.

"Never mind, Araf. I will be here for a few weeks before I go back to Sittwe. We've got all these new houses to build."

New houses! Does this mean the people of Eight Quarters District are on their way home? Could she ask the truck driver? But before she can decide, Araf does it for her.

"Who are you building new houses for?"

"The people coming to live here, of course." Zaw Gyi smiles again. "Hey, please wait," he says, before climbing into his cab and returning with a box of tamarind jaggery. "Here you are." He offers Araf one of the sweet-sour drops, and then holds the box out to Cat Girl and finally Hasina. Should she take one? He seems so nice—why does she feel uncertain about him?

"I have a friend with a teashop. He could use a boy like you. You could make enough money to buy your own truck."

Hasina shudders on the inside. But outside, she pulls Araf closer to her and then bows low, giving Zaw Gyi a respectful *shi-kho*. "Thank you for the jaggery. We must go now."

"Okay. Bye, Araf."

Hasina hauls Araf and Cat Girl away. The men in hard hats were building new houses, not for those who used to live here, but for new people. If someone built a new house on your old land, how would you get it back? She doesn't know the answer. And right now, she has other worries.

This harvest, there is no Nurzamal to work out when the crop is ready. No neighbors to help. Only a sick old lady, a little kid, a girl with a limp, and Hasina. Still, she hopes that if they can bring in even a small harvest, then they will have food for the months to come. Rice, oil, salt: the basics of any home in Myanmar.

Hasina hurries Araf and the Cat Girl along. Dadi and Ghadiya are far in the distance, just past the construction village where the land dips away to the paddy fields. Hasina can see them, two small figures passing a couple of battered blue nylon tents.

"Come on, you two."

The closer Hasina gets to the paddy field, the more suspicious those blue tents look to her. They are close enough to the construction village to be part of it, yet they look like they don't belong with those shiny trucks and busy men in hard hats. Did these tents belong to the kidnappers the kind Arakanese man has warned her about?

Hasina takes a good look at the tents as she approaches them, Araf and Cat Girl close behind her.

Someone inside unzips a flap. Hasina can see a dark eye watching them through the mesh.

"Hello?" she calls out in Rohingya, her voice firm rather than friendly, then *"Mingalar bar."* The person inside zips the flap up fast.

"Come on," Hasina says to Araf and Cat Girl, hurrying the others past this strange behavior.

They drop down onto one of the sandy paths that crisscross the paddy fields. The rice plants are deep green, the tops golden in color and bending over with their own weight. Anyone can see that it is time to harvest. But these fields are farmed by the people of Eight Quarters and they are all gone.

Up ahead at the edge of the paddy fields, Hasina can

see a little knot of people. Dadi Asmah, Ghadiya, and a man. Is this another driver? As she draws closer, she sees the man is in uniform. He is thickset, his *longyi* tied up tight. He has a clipboard and a smirk on his face.

"What's happening?" she whispers to Ghadiya when they join them.

"The watchman won't let us go to our land," Ghadiya replies.

"What are they saying?" Araf asks, for his grand-mother and the watchman are speaking rapid Burmese.

Hasina translates. "This is my land, Dadi Asmah is telling the man. The crop will go to waste."

"Can you prove this is your land? You look like a foreigner." Except the watchman uses the word *kalama*.

"This is my land. It has been my land for genera-tions."

Dadi Asmah's back is straight. Her voice is clear and low. Gone is the sick body, racked by hunger and all those days walking through the woods. Gone is the croaky voice that so frightened Hasina when her grandmother first returned. Instead, Dadi Asmah is a determined woman using all her strength to stand up to this man.

"Many of your kind have run away. How do I know you are not stealing someone else's crop?"

"I want to harvest my rice. You can see the fields are full. You can see that the rice will spoil. If the rice spoils, this land will be no good. Who will do the work? You?"

The man blinks a little.

"We all have to eat, my friend. I am an old woman. Allow me to feed myself and my grandchildren."

The man looks embarrassed. It is not normal for

young men to be cruel to old women, to be discourteous. And yet, these are not normal times. He looks down to his clipboard. "Many foreigners are stealing the rice from the land," he mutters. "You cannot harvest until I see proof that the land is yours."

Stealing crops? This land—all of this land—has been farmed by the residents of Eight Quarters District since before Hasina's father was even born. In all the years she's been to her family's harvests, no one has ever needed proof of ownership.

"And when I bring proof?"

"Then you may harvest."

Dadi Asmah gives the man a shallow *shi-kho*, then turns, her back straight as she walks along the path. "Come, Hasina, Ghadiya. Araf. Cat Girl."

Cat Girl slips her thin arm around Dadi Asmah's waist. In single file they climb up the bank onto the spit of land, passing the nylon tents. Again, the zip whizzes as Hasina passes. Again, a pair of dark eyes peers out at them.

"What do you want?" Hasina growls at the eyes, and the zip whizzes closed again.

As they trudge back past the construction workers setting up their village, Hasina falls into step beside her grandmother. "The truck driver told us that the men are here to build houses for people moving *in*, not moving *back*."

Dadi Asmah sighs. "They're trying to starve us out and drive us away. But we can't let them, Hasina, can we?"

CHAPTER 22

Now it is always the same questions that run through Hasina's mind. *How will I feed my family? How will I get permission to harvest our rice? How will I prove the land and rice belong to us?* She talks them over with Isak at the bazaar.

"Even if you do get permission, how are you going to harvest a crop with a sick old lady and a bunch of small children? You will need help."

Isak is mending a puppet of a horse. The horse is charming. It makes Hasina happy but sad too—it reminds her of all they have lost. Isak spins the horse around on its strings and makes it gallop to Hasina, as if to say, *I will help, if you let me.* Isak's shoulder is stronger, but he still limps. She would like to ask him. But a girl asking a boy? What will he think of her if she asks for help? Maybe he won't think of her as strong and clever anymore. Some things she can't bring herself to do.

"Dadi Asmah seems to have forgotten all about the land anyway."

It was true. Dadi Asmah has taken to her room. She has become sick and old again. That dry cough has returned and she eats even less. The cousins are so concerned that Ghadiya stays home with Asmah while Hasina and Araf go to the bazaar, even though Uncle Rashid has told them to stay together. Asmah just sits in her room, opening her old books and flipping through the pages one by one. She reaches into the drawers of her bureau, taking things out and putting them back in again. It is as if she is trying to reach back into the past. As if she has given up the fight. As if her words at the paddy fields—*we can't let them*—meant nothing. As if once again, it is up to Hasina to make sure they eat.

Meanwhile, the rice grains thicken on the stem. Harvest should have begun by now. The rice will go yellow if they cannot prove to the watchman at the paddy field that the land is theirs. Nobody wins if the crop is lost.

Hasina too has been examining a book. Specifically, the high school math textbook in Aunt Rukiah's room. Hasina has always loved its green covers, the smell of the ink off the pages. Once upon a time, she promised herself that she would learn how to do all the problems in that textbook. Now, she sees it in another way. How much is it worth? How much rice can it buy?

But the book is not hers to sell. It is Aunt Rukiah's precious possession. One evening when Hasina picks the book up, weighing it in her hand like a packet of lentils, Ghadiya turns on her. "That is my mother's. Do not touch it."

If Ghadiya won't let her sell it, then what? If she's honest, Hasina would rather not sell the textbook but keep it, if only for selfish reasons. For Ghadiya, it is her mother's precious possession. For Hasina, the education she will never have. But what are they to eat? Soon, very soon, they will run out of what the Arakanese man gave them.

When Rashid phones, Hasina tells him of their plight. "Uncle, we have no money and little food. Can you help us?"

Rashid promises to send them money. The question is, how? He will have to find someone with a bank account who is willing to help. Even if he offers a fee, right now no one feels safe helping a Rohingya. "It will take a little bit of time," he apologizes.

Time is what they do not have. Time is how much rice is left in the bottom of a bag. Time is the pinching of hunger in the belly.

One good thing is that Aunt Rukiah has phoned Rashid. "She is in the Kutapalong camp," he tells Ghadiya. "She misses you and loves you very much."

Ghadiya's eyes shine with tears of pure joy. She is so ecstatic she hugs the nearest person, who just happens to be Araf. "Mama is alive and well!" she sings.

"Mmmhmmmm!" Araf shouts grouchily.

Hasina too feels a rare moment of joy. She loves her aunt Rukiah. And besides, if Aunt Rukiah has been found, does that mean there is word of her parents too?

"Sorry, Hasina, there is no firm news of your parents. They were separated at the crossing of the River Naf.

But she has heard that there are more people from Eight Quarters in another part of the camp. She will find them. We must be patient."

Hasina feels she has been nothing but patient.

One afternoon at the bazaar Araf announces that he has seen Zaw Gyi, the too-friendly truck driver, helping U Ko Yin. "He is outside U Ko Yin's teashop right now."

"You want to be careful of U Ko Yin," Isak warns. Today, he has a puppet *nagar*, which he has been making dance for Araf. "You better show me this Zaw Gyi, so I can see him for myself."

Isak creeps over with Araf. "There he was," Isak reports back to Hasina, "just like you described him, sticky-out ears and rumpled hair, and couch potato *longyi*—crumpled at the hem. We watched him deliver bags of rice and boxes of medicines marked *AID*— foreigners" gifts to help our people—to U Ko Yin's teashop."

"So, the driver and U Ko Yin know each other," Hasina murmurs.

"Yes, they do. And if the driver knows U Ko Yin, then you can bet he is up to no good. Araf," Isak says, his voice serious, "you keep away from U Ko Yin's teashop. And that driver too."

"But he has such a lovely truck!" Araf wails.

It is a few weeks after the trip to the paddy fields when Hasina returns home from the bazaar to find Dadi Asmah waiting for her, a wide smile on her face. "I've got them," she says.

Asmah opens up a faded photograph album. At the front of the album are papers with English writing on them—Hasina recognizes the letters, though she cannot read them. Dadi Asmah keeps turning pages until she comes to pictures of a girl. A girl with long braided hair and a hawk-like nose. The girl is Asmah.

There are many pictures of Dadi Asmah as a girl. There's one in which the brick house, the one they are in now, is being built. There she is at school, the Anglican Girls School. Hasina recognizes the building as the Basic Education School, where she so wished she could study. But it is the picture of the paddy field that has got her grandmother excited. Here is Dadi Asmah as a young girl during the harvest.

"These photographs are proof that this is my land. Tomorrow we go back. Tomorrow we harvest our rice."

<hr />

The next day Dadi Asmah is ready early. They eat the last of their rice cooked into a thin gruel. It is barely enough to take the edge off the morning hunger, but it must do for breakfast, lunch, and dinner. Hasina hopes against hope that Dadi Asmah is right and that they will be able to begin the harvest today.

Asmah marches them past the trucks, where the bulldozers are flattening out the piles of ash that were once houses. Men in hard hats read from plans, gesticulating here and there. Workmen in singlets and *longyi*s position blue pipes in long rows. She marches them past the nylon tents, with their occupants zipping open the flaps to spy on them. She marches them right up to the watchman.

"*Mingalar bar*," she says in perfect Burmese, bowing her head.

"*Mingalar bar*," the watchman returns nervously, his clipboard at the ready.

"If you do not let us harvest this land, these children will die. This child"—Dadi Asmah gestures to Araf— "will not eat again until the harvest is in. We want only what is ours. The rice is ready to be harvested. The grains are bursting. It is a sin to let this food go to waste."

Hasina watches her grandmother, with her straight back and her head held up, show first one photograph and then the next. The watchman shakes his head, scribbling notes on his clipboard. But it is when Dadi Asmah produces the notes in English that he takes notice. Meekly, he copies down the words that he does not know. And then, he lets them pass.

Dadi Asmah turns and shoots Hasina a sparkling smile. "The crop, my children, is ready for harvest."

Hasina stands up and stretches. Her back aches. The sun is burning hot. Already she needs a drink. Ahead of her, Dadi Asmah, Araf, and Ghadiya are plodding slowly through the paddy. Hasina looks across the field. There are so many more rice plants to go.

They have been harvesting the rice for three days. It is not as easy as Hasina had hoped. It is tiring to bend over all day long and cut the paddy into bunches. Too much for Dadi Asmah, who is fading after the effort of standing up to the watchman. The heat too is sapping her grandmother's strength. Ghadiya is finding it difficult with her limp to keep going in the water. Only Cat Girl can almost keep up with Hasina—she is as quick with her hands, and lithe as well.

By Dhurh on the first day, they are all done in, and must spend the hottest part of the day resting in a shaded spot. It doesn't help that they are working on empty stomachs. Hasina hoped to have a harvest in three days, but now, she knows it will take so much longer. How they will do it without food, she doesn't know.

It doesn't help either that the watchman keeps his beady gaze on them, pretending to note when they come and go on his clipboard. Or that the people of the tent keep watching them as well, the whizz of their tent flap zipping open now a familiar sound.

Over the next three days they trudge along the spit of land where the construction workers have set up their village. Each day the workers erase more of what were once homes. Each day the bulldozers push the ash into the soil, and along with it the pots and pans and clothes and posters and spectacles and shoes and toys, those things that remain from those burnt-out houses. When the soil is brown again, the men wrap string around bamboo sticks wedged into the soil, measuring out squares and rectangles that will be new houses.

Hasina feels unbearably sad to see those little sticks with their twists of string rise so quickly. It is as if all those families, all those children, never existed. Never felt hunger or love or warmth or anger or happiness. As if their lives were nothing.

It makes her feel so hopeless. It doesn't help that the harvest is taking so much longer than she'd expected. Each day they seem to get less done than the day before.

Hunger is part of it. Today, all that any of them has eaten is tea made from the last twists of wild ginger and a bit of fish they caught yesterday. Araf has already complained that he is hungry, and Hasina snapped at him and sent him on ahead with Dadi. Ghadiya too has quarreled with her. They have all been working so hard that at night they have no strength to gather any food. Hunger gnaws at her insides.

On the fourth morning, as Hasina stretches her aching back, a familiar figure lopes along the path.

"Isak!" Araf shouts.

"I heard you could do with some help," Isak calls to Asmah, smiling his crinkly smile.

"Yes, we can." She smiles back.

"Isak," Hasina chides, her face pink with embarrassment, "I didn't ask you to come."

"No," Isak admits, "Araf did." The two boys wink at each other.

The first thing Isak does is find a shady spot for Dadi Asmah to rest. Then he joins Hasina, standing tall beside her.

"What can I do?" he asks. But even with Isak, the going is slow. Hunger isn't the only thing holding them back. Hasina cannot help but remember the harvests of old. Painful memories of her mother taking gifts of rice and blue ducks eggs to her neighbors in Third Mile and the bazaar. Even if they do succeed in bringing in their crop, who will they share it with? Mama and Baba are still only shadows in a faraway camp. And their friends, their neighbors, are all gone.

Early on the fifth morning, they file past the construction village before dropping down into the paddy field. An old woman, a small boy, a limping girl, a wounded teenager, Cat Girl, and Hasina bringing up the rear.

Five days already, Hasina thinks, and still so much to go. They are surviving on wild guavas now. She pauses by the blue tents to calculate how much longer, watching as the others pick their way through the field. Cat Girl waits by her side.

"Don't worry," Cat Girl says in her broken Burmese. And then, she says something in Mro that sounds like "*hom, tui.*"

There's the familiar whizz of the zip. But instead of an eye peeking out, this time the front flap of the tent itself opens and a tiny woman emerges.

The woman is not interested in Hasina. Instead, she speaks directly to Cat Girl, who drops Hasina's hand and cries out, then speaks back rapidly in the same language.

Then the tiny woman addresses Hasina in faltering Burmese. "This girl," she says, "she is Mro-*cha*. She is from our people, the humans, or Mro."

The woman beckons Hasina to her tent. She pulls back the flap and calls into the tent. Inside is a man, another woman, and three children. "Mro-*cha*," she says. "Husband. Older sister. Children."

All the way through the paddy field Cat Girl chatters happily with the woman. When they catch up with the others, it is the older sister who speaks in Mro while the woman, who introduces herself as Lama, translates. "We have seen you with this Mro-*cha*. You saved her. You are kind to her. We wanted to speak to you because you are kind."

Lama purses her lips in sorrow. "Many of my people have been killed. Some by ARSA. Others by the AA."

Then Lama turns to Cat Girl and asks her a few questions. "She says that they left the village because men came, men with guns. But when they were at the river, different men came. These had knives. She says there were many people in the forest, not just Mro-*cha*. Others, walking. She says that you"—here Lama looks at Dadi Asmah—"are kind and helped her. For that, we Mro-*cha* thank you.

"We too have had to leave our village. Bad men came to punish us. They thought we were Buddhists who had killed their Muslim friends. There is no one left in our village now."

Dadi Asmah tuts. "Always, the story is the same. Bad men come, and who suffers?"

But Lama isn't done. "We are hungry."

"We have no food to offer," Dadi Asmah apologizes.

"No," says Lama. "But you have rice to harvest. And we can help."

They begin soon afterward. Lama insists that Dadi Asmah rest in the shade. Hasina is glad of this. The harvest has taken a serious toll on her grandmother, who is moving painfully slowly and often has to stop what she is doing because of a coughing fit.

So, the paddy is cut. It is beaten against the wooden frames, the grains falling like rain on the plastic sheet spread to catch them. And then the rice is winnowed, thrown up in the air in a swirling motion so that the light husk blows away but the heavy rice falls back onto the tray. In two days, the field is cleared and rice is spread on cloths to dry in the sun. After four days, a dozen plump bags of rice sit ready. Some for the Mro-*cha* to store in their nylon tent, some for Hasina to put away. Some for Isak to keep in his room behind the Brothers & Sons Puppet Stall.

Hasina cannot help but grin. Satisfaction flows through her. No more starvation! How proud she feels, with the crop harvested and two families fed. Three if you count Isak. If only her mother were here to see it. Tonight, they will all sleep well, knowing that breakfast will be substantial. The only worry is that Dadi Asmah's skin is tighter across her face. But rest and good food will make her grandmother look less drawn. It will make all of them feel good. Hasina could not be more satisfied.

It is at the edge of the paddy field that Lama stops and takes Cat Girl by the hand. She bends and whispers to the girl, who nods.

Lama turns to Hasina. "She will stay with us now."

And then Lama turns and gives Asmah a deep *shi-kho*. "We will take care of her."

Cat Girl hugs Hasina, Ghadiya, and Asmah. She bows to Isak. But it is only when she comes to Araf that she cries. Poor Araf goes quite red and looks like he might cry too. And then with a zip of the nylon flap, Cat Girl is with her own people again.

"I miss Cat Girl." Araf sighs, to everyone's surprise.

"Cat Girl has Lama's family now," Ghadiya murmurs. "She will be happy."

"Yes," says Isak, "but how much she must long for her own mother and father. And they are gone forever."

Poor Isak, Hasina thinks. How she misses her baba and mama. Food is one thing, but love is another. All it would take to make Hasina's happiness complete would be to hear from Rashid that her parents have been found.

CHAPTER 23

The call comes long after they have gone to bed.

Ghadiya answers the hand phone. Hasina can hear her cousin's voice go from sleepy to excited in two short words.

"Hello? Daddy? I'll get her." Ghadiya turns to Hasina. "He wants to talk to you."

Hasina holds the phone to her ear. Is this what she's been waiting for? Have her parents been found? Is it good news or bad?

Uncle Rashid wastes no time. His voice is full of energy. "Hasina? I can't speak long. I am waiting for a call from the refugee camp. But I have good news. Your parents have been found."

"Where are they?"

Beside her, Araf stirs and wakes. "What is it? What is going on?"

"Uncle Rashid has found Mama and Baba!"

Ghadiya tumbles out of the bed. "I will go and get Dadi."

Hasina puts an arm around Araf, who snuggles into her side. She holds the phone between their ears so they can both hear.

"Ibrahim and Nurzamal are with Rukiah at the camp," Rashid continues. "They are safe and, I believe, they are well."

"How do you know?"

"Rukiah found them. And then a non-government organization called me. The NGO workers are trying to arrange for your parents to phone you. It will be in a few days. Now, I must go, Hasina—there's another call coming through. But the news is good."

"I will tell Dadi—"

But Rashid has already hung up.

Hasina and Araf hug each other tight. Their parents are alive. Alive! At last, they have real news. Hasina doesn't know whether to laugh or cry. How long has it been since she last spoke to her parents? She adds up the days and weeks into months. She has yearned for just this news. What will it feel like to speak to her mother again? Wait until she hears about the rice harvest! What will it feel like to speak to her father? Will he be pleased with her? Has she done the right thing by her brother and cousin and grandmother? She thinks back to the terrible night of the men like demons, to the last time she saw her parents. She doesn't even feel like the same person.

Araf, as usual, is full of questions. "When will they come home? Do they miss me? Where exactly are they? Will they bring me a present? Oh, when are they coming home?"

Hasina laughs. "Of course they miss you, Araf. But you can ask them yourself. Uncle Rashid says they will call in a few days."

Just then, Ghadiya returns to the room.

"Ghadiya, your mother has found Baba and Mama. They are all in a camp in Bangladesh. Did you tell Dadi Asmah?"

But Ghadiya's face is anxious. "Hasina, I can't wake Dadi."

Hasina feels a stab of fear. Quickly, she pads across to her grandmother's room, Ghadiya and Araf behind her.

Asmah looks tiny and frail beneath her thin coverlet. In the moonlight, her face is gray.

"Dadi," Hasina whispers, "we have good news. Wake up!"

But Dadi Asmah does not wake up.

"Dadi?" Hasina places her hand on her grandmother's forehead. Her skin is clammy and hot. Gently, she shakes Asmah's shoulder. "Dadi? Wake up, Dadi. Uncle Rashid has found Baba and Mama!"

Asmah sighs, but doesn't open her eyes.

"Please, Dadi." Hasina is about to grip her by the shoulder again when something strange happens to her grandmother's body.

Asmah begins to shake. Her whole body shivers, her teeth chatter, her legs rattle. The shivering lasts for a long minute before she is still again.

"That is what Araf looked like when he had the fever," Ghadiya whispers.

Hasina stares at her cousin. Ghadiya is right—this looks like fever. Which means that Dadi Asmah needs medicine, and she needs it now.

But there is only one place Hasina can think of to get what Asmah needs: U Ko Yin's shop at the bazaar.

CHAPTER 24

Just before the first light, when the watchman opens up the steel doors, Hasina and Araf arrive at the bazaar entrance to wait. Under one arm, Hasina carries a heavy parcel. This is the only thing left of value in their home—Aunt Rukiah's textbook.

"Come on, Araf," Hasina whispers, taking his hand and rushing him through the silent bazaar as soon as the doors are opened. When they rattle the steel roller door at the Brothers & Sons Puppet Stall, a sleepy Isak pokes his head under the bottom.

"Isak," Hasina whispers, "oh Isak, Dadi Asmah has fever and I need medicine fast."

Isak rolls up the door to his room and invites them onto the platform. "What can I do to help?"

"I need to buy medicine from U Ko Yin. Can I leave Araf with you?"

"I can do better than that. We will go together. I don't like you talking to that man alone."

Hasina would like to say no, but the truth is, she

feels safer with Isak at her back. The three of them walk toward U Ko Yin's stall.

Hasina stops in a sheltered spot just before they get there. She gives Araf a quick hug. "Please be patient and wait here with Isak while I talk to U Ko Yin. Thank you, Isak."

"Don't worry. I will be right here."

Hasina takes half a dozen steps toward U Ko Yin's stall. Up ahead, U Ko Yin is fussing around a new delivery of rice and medicines. And who should be wheeling it in, but Zaw Gyi from the construction village. At the sight of him, Hasina's heart lurches and she shrinks into the shadows, waiting until the bags of rice are piled up and Zaw Gyi has gone. Then, with her heart in her mouth, she prepares to speak to U Ko Yin.

"Uncle?" she calls in a small voice.

But U Ko Yin is too busy writing on a white card with a red pen, making a sign advertising his new stock.

"Uncle?" Hasina repeats, this time louder.

U Ko Yin turns and grimaces. "Oh, it is you," he grunts.

Hasina *shi-kho*s deeply before him. "Uncle, may I—"

"I am busy right now, Hasina. Come back later."

"Sorry, Uncle." Her voice feels very small. "Uncle, my grandmother is very sick."

"Humph," U Ko Yin grunts, busy with his sign.

"I need some medicine for her. Please, Uncle. How much? For medicine?"

At the magic words *how much*, U Ko Yin's ears prick up. He swivels around and gives Hasina his best salesman's smile. "Very good medicine. Foreigners' medicine. Special price for you. Ten thousand kyats."

Ten thousand kyats! It is a fortune. And whether it's ten thousand or two thousand, Hasina doesn't have it. All she has is in the parcel.

"Uncle, I have no money, but I do have this." She unwraps the math book that Aunt Rukiah brought all the way from her school in the south. Thick, heavy, full of the numbers that Hasina loves so much. It is a wrench, but she holds the book out to U Ko Yin.

"A book! A book!" U Ko Yin laughs. "What do I want with a book? It is in English! Not even in Myanmar language. You will have to find something I want, if you must trade for your medicines." His eyes narrow. "I have told you—your boy, he should be working. I can get him a job. Not at my teashop, mind you, but another one. Then you can have all the medicines you need."

"Araf is too young."

"Your choice," retorts U Ko Yin. "But too bad for your grandmother."

"Please, Uncle. Is there nothing else …"

U Ko Yin ignores her. He is finished with her.

Utterly miserable, Hasina turns to trudge back to Isak and Araf. She feels like weeping, but what good would it do?

Araf launches himself from the shadows. Isak follows close behind.

"Did you get medicine for Dadi Asmah?"

"No."

"No?" exclaims Araf. "Why not?"

"He wants ten thousand kyats."

"Give him the money."

"I don't have it, Araf."

"What about the book?"

"He doesn't want a math book, he wants money or …"

"Or what?"

"Or nothing. Forget U Ko Yin. We will find another way."

"What way?" Araf demands.

Hasina doesn't have an answer.

Before she can stop him, Araf pulls away from her and sprints straight toward U Ko Yin. He tugs at his *longyi* to get his attention.

"Please. My dadi must have medicine. I will do anything."

"Anything? Now we are talking," U Ko Yin replies, his voice oily. He shoots Hasina a triumphant grin. "Would you like a nice job in a teashop? The pay is all the medicine you need. Good medicine, from foreigners."

"I will work in your teashop."

"No, Araf!" Hasina cries out in horror.

"Let the boy speak for himself."

Isak steps forward. His dark eyes flash with defiance.

"Araf, come here." Isak grabs Araf's arm and pulls the boy to his side. "You leave him alone, U Ko Yin, he is only a boy. He will not work for you."

U Ko Yin shrugs his shoulders and smiles his insincere smile. "We will see about that."

Tears flow down Araf's face as Hasina and Isak march him back to the family stall.

"Araf," Isak speaks gently, "the boys who work in teashops are stolen from their families. They are treated very badly."

"But what about Dadi?" he wails.

"We will think of something," Hasina replies. "But please, stay here," she begs.

"Don't worry, he is safe with me," Isak promises.

Hasina unwraps the precious math book. This is her last chance. She walks to the Arakanese part of the market. She sees a woman opening her stall.

Shyly Hasina approaches her. "*Mingalar bar*," she begins, in Burmese. "My grandmother is very sick. I need ten thousand kyats to buy medicine. I am selling this math textbook." The woman looks at Hasina in surprise. She narrows her eyes and shakes her head.

Hasina tries stall after stall. Nobody wants to speak to, let alone buy from, a Rohingya. One man shouts at her, "Ask your own kind for help." Another takes pity on her, and gives her a packet of sweets. But that is all.

After an hour, Hasina still does not have money or medicines. She is about to return to the family stall when she spots the kind Arakanese man. She has come full circle in the market.

"Please!" she calls to him.

He stops, turning to face her, and Hasina takes a few faltering steps toward him. "Please, you have been so kind to us. I want to ask you for one more kindness. My grandmother is very ill." She gets no farther before hot tears pour from her eyes and her voice shakes. "I need ten thousand kyats to buy medicine. I have no money. I am selling this math textbook."

"Ten thousand kyats?"

"She has fever. U Ko Yin has foreign medicine."

"What kind of medicine?"

"Tablets."

"Like these?" The Arakanese man fishes a shiny packet of pills from his pocket.

"Yes," she cries, her heart leaping with hope. "Like those!"

The kind Arakanese man turns to his stall and pulls out a metal box. Inside are more shiny packets full of pills in different colors and sizes.

"You said fever?"

"Yes."

"Then, she needs to take these morning, noon, evening, and bedtime." He hands her a silver packet before fishing out another, this time with green and white capsules. "And these too, once a day, with her breakfast. By the way, we sell the fever medicine for two hundred kyats not ten thousand. These others, two hundred and fifty."

"Thank you." She *shi-kho*s to the kind man and then hands him the book.

"You keep your book," he says.

"But I must repay you."

The kind Arakanese man sighs. It's a sound both sad and weary. "We've seen such bad things. There is nothing to be paid. Just stay away from U Ko Yin."

Hasina sprints back to their stall, relief flooding through her. She holds the precious slab of medicines in her fingers. *Get Araf*, she plans. *Thank Isak*—Isak, who is always there when she needs him. *Get home. Give Dadi the medicine.* Quickly, quickly, she repeats this in her head.

But when she gets to the stall, Isak is slumped on the ground. And Araf is nowhere to be seen.

"Isak!" Hasina cries. "Are you okay?"

Isak groans. "Hasina?" He lifts his hand to his head. "Ouch."

Hasina can see a large swelling rising on Isak's skull. "You're hurt! What happened?"

"Someone hit me from behind." He touches his scalp gingerly. "Where's Araf?"

Hasina feels the warmth drain from her body. She checks behind the curtains. No Araf. She rushes back to Isak's side. Her foot hits a white package on the floor, neatly tied.

As soon as she sees the packet, Hasina feels that dead weight in her stomach. She picks it up and unwraps it with trembling fingers. Inside, there are several boxes of foreigners" medicine stamped *AID* in red. There's also a bit of paper. In red ink are the words *10,000 kyats— received in kind.*

"Isak, look at this!"

Isak takes the paper from her hand. "It's a bill of sale." He looks up at Hasina. "U Ko Yin has Araf. He has bought him."

Hasina turns and runs to U Ko Yin's stall. U Ko Yin is writing more signs in the same red pen.

"Uncle," she says to U Ko Yin, "I found these medicines."

U Ko Yin looks up at her. He smiles a nasty smile. "I told you, you can have all the medicines you need. As long as I get what I need."

"Where is Araf?" she demands.

"He asked me to find him work."

"He's too young!" she shouts.

"Your kind shouldn't be shouting in the bazaar. People will think you're causing trouble."

"Where is Araf, please?" Hasina begs.

"You should be thinking about your sick grandmother. Araf is thinking of her. You don't have much time if she has fever."

Hasina peers beyond U Ko Yin's shoulder and into his empty teashop. She steps around him, searching beyond the tables.

"You won't find him here! I told you—he will have a job, but not in my shop."

"Give him back! Please! I beg you."

"Araf has decided. The deal is made and a contract is a contract. If I were you, I would go home to your grandmother. Give her the medicines while they can still make a difference."

CHAPTER 25

Hasina runs the whole way back. How have things got this bad? She must get the medicine to Dadi. But if she does, how will she find Araf? If she searches for Araf, how will she get the medicine to Dadi? By the time she gets back to the stall, color has returned to Isak's face and he is sitting up.

"Where is Araf?"

She hangs her head. "U Ko Yin has him."

"No!" Isak groans.

"I don't know what to do, Isak. I need to get medicine home to Dadi. But I also need to find Araf."

"This is all my fault. Let me help you. Please, Hasina. Let me look for Araf."

"But your head."

Isak gives himself a shake. "I'm fine. Look, if U Ko Yin has Araf, then Araf must still be here in the bazaar. Nobody knows this place like I do. It's the least I can do. You take the medicine to your grandmother."

"But—"

"Go!" he commands. "I will find Araf and bring him back to you."

Hasina arrives back at Third Mile Street just as Dadi Asmah is having one of her shivering fits. Ghadiya is putting a cool compress to her head.

Hasina holds up the pills from the kind Arakanese man. "I have medicine. She needs these morning, lunch, evening, and bedtime. And these, at night and in the morning. Then, we have to wait."

Together, Ghadiya and Hasina rouse Dadi. They give her the medicine. When her body begins to cool and she seems more peaceful, Hasina pulls her cousin aside.

"We have another problem," Hasina whispers to her cousin. "A very bad problem. U Ko Yin has Araf."

"What!" Ghadiya exclaims.

"I think he's taking him to work in a teashop somewhere. Isak is looking for him at the bazaar. I am going back there now."

Hasina places U Ko Yin's box of medicines on the bed. She explains how she tried to trade the math textbook for this medicine. How U Ko Yin had wanted ten thousand kyats and then, how he wanted Araf to work for him. How Araf has said he would work for U Ko Yin. How the medicines were worth far less than U Ko Yin was asking. How Isak had been knocked out and Araf taken.

"Poor Araf, he is trying to help," Ghadiya cries.

Just then, there is a call from outside. Hasina's heart

lifts. *Isak is here.* But when the cousins run outside, they find Isak alone.

"I searched everywhere. I asked the stallholders. Nothing," Isak says, miserable. "This is all my fault."

"They knocked you out, Isak."

"I think we need help. Adult help," Ghadiya interjects.

Hasina agrees. But who can they turn to? The kind Arakanese stallholder? But he has already given her medicines. Would he really stick his neck out for a Rohingya against another stallholder, even though it is U Ko Yin?

"So, he is not in U Ko Yin's shop, not even in the back room?" Ghadiya asks.

"He wasn't there," Isak replies.

"U Ko Yin was very clear—he will not be working in *his* teashop. He will be working in *a* teashop," Hasina says.

"Tell me exactly what you saw this morning while we were waiting for you near U Ko Yin's stall," Isak says to Hasina.

"U Ko Yin was unloading rice. The rice with the red stamp—you said it is a gift to us from foreigners. I remember that, because Zaw Gyi was delivering it."

"Zaw Gyi?" Isak says. "The truck driver with the messy hair? I saw him hanging around. It must have been him who knocked me out."

Something clicks together in Hasina's brain then. It is like the day of the helicopters, when she could just *see* what she needed to do. "What if Zaw Gyi is delivering the boys … Think about it: the first time we met him, he invited Araf to climb into the cab of his truck."

"He said he could find him a job. *In a teashop*," Ghadiya exclaims. "And he brings in the AID rice and medicines. He must go back and forth to Sittwe all the time."

"So Zaw Gyi has Araf."

Then Hasina remembers Uncle Rashid's words. *If you need help, call this number.* "The Rohingya lawyer," she says. "He is in Sittwe."

Ghadiya fetches the hand phone and taps in the number that Rashid told her to write down. The phone rings. Ghadiya puts it on speaker. The three of them lean over the screen.

"*Aasso-lamu alaikum*?" a voice answers.

"Hello?" Hasina responds with utter relief. "My uncle Rashid said to call you if I need help."

"I am the lawyer Hann Linn. Please go on."

Hasina tells the lawyer about Araf, the truck driver, and U Ko Yin's words. "And so, you see," she finishes, "I think Araf has been taken to work at a teashop. But he is too young to make such decisions. He should not have to go."

"My dear, I will try to help you, but I am in Sittwe. I cannot come to you and you do not have much time. If you cannot find your brother before he leaves Teknadaung, even though right is on your side, he may well be impossible to trace. He will disappear somewhere. Always moving, always just ahead of you. You must find him *now*, before he is taken from Teknadaung."

As they end the call, Hasina feels that old, familiar stone in the belly. "How am I going to find him?" she asks Isak and Ghadiya.

"The truck!" Ghadiya exclaims. "Zaw Gyi is always hanging around the bazaar or his truck."

It makes sense. If Araf isn't at the bazaar, he will be somewhere in or near Zaw Gyi's truck.

"Do we know where the truck is?" Isak asks.

"Yes," says Hasina, her voice determined. "He parks it in the construction workers" village. I know where. And that is where I am going now."

"And I will be right beside you."

CHAPTER 26

Hasina runs along Third Mile Street like she used to run along the back field waiting for the ball. Her head is clear. She has one thing on her mind. *Find Araf.* She and Isak turn for the path along the river. In another twenty minutes, they are in the construction village at the bottom of Eight Quarters District.

The village is once more transformed. The workers have finished laying out the new houses—those string rectangles tied around little wooden stakes indicating rooms and doors. Now, there is a new level of activity as men shift the materials to build the houses. Bales of wire are being rolled from the backs of trucks. Men are pushing wheelbarrows of sand and gravel, sawing planks, hammering nails. There are more men, and there is more equipment, and there are more trucks.

There are so many more trucks now that she cannot see the big red truck with a blue peacock and *Sittwe Transport* painted on the side. What if Zaw Gyi is not here after all?

"You go that way," she tells Isak. "Look for a blue peacock and *Sittwe Transport*."

For what feels like ages, she runs along the rows of parked trucks, searching for the Sittwe truck.

At last she sees it, and she seems to be in luck. There is no sign of Zaw Gyi here at all. She can have a good look at the truck and find Araf.

First she tries the driver's side, but it is locked. Then she tries the passenger side, but it too is locked. She peers inside. No sign of Araf. But what if he is down behind the seat? What if he is hidden? She bangs her fist on the window.

"Araf?" she shouts through the glass. "Araf!"

And then a hand grabs her by the ankle.

Hasina kicks and kicks. The hand lets go. She jumps off the truck, ready to run, but from under the truck peeks a familiar face.

"*Isak?*" she whispers.

There's the crunch of a footstep.

"Quick, get under here."

Down they roll, she and Isak, until they are below the truck side by side. This is the closest Hasina has ever been to Isak. She can feel his long legs beside hers, his strong arms. She is glad that he is here. It makes her feel braver not to be alone.

They have hidden just in the nick of time. From underneath the truck, Hasina can see the crumpled hem of a brown *longyi*.

Zaw Gyi is whistling a happy tune. He opens the

truck cabin, rummages around, then closes it again and walks off.

Araf, then, is not in the truck cabin.

Hasina turns her face to Isak, about to ask, "Where is Araf?" when Isak pushes his hand over her mouth. Zaw Gyi hasn't walked away. He is walking around the truck, to the back. Hasina holds her breath. Is that where Araf is? In the cargo box behind the cab where the goods are carried? She listens intently for sounds of Araf struggling.

The driver clambers inside and walks through, each step making the chassis bounce right above their heads. Hasina can almost feel his big flat feet on her face.

Zaw Gyi thumps back along the truck bed and then springs off and lands heavily on the ground. He pushes and pulls at something before shutting the roller door with a clatter.

But still he doesn't leave. He paces up and down at the back of the truck, whistling his cheerful tune.

And then, another pair of feet appear at the rear of the truck. Another *longyi*, this one neatly pressed.

"Where to with this lot, boss?" Zaw Gyi asks in Burmese.

"Golden Teashop, Sittwe," the voice says.

Hasina recognizes that voice.

"Do you want to inspect the merchandise?" Zaw Gyi asks.

"No. You do your job, I do mine. Just make sure

they get enough water. We don't want any more deaths, *la*. Not good for business."

Finally, the two men walk off.

Hasina and Isak exchange a long look. She was right. Araf *is* in the truck. In fact, he is probably only a few centimeters above them.

"Golden Teashop, Sittwe," Isak repeats. "That was U Ko Yin, I am sure of it," he adds, and Hasina nods.

Her fears were justified. U Ko Yin and Zaw Gyi work together. They have taken Araf and sold him to the Golden Teashop in Sittwe.

Sittwe is the capital of Rakhine, a big city. That is a good hour's drive. If Zaw Gyi succeeds in getting Araf there, Araf will be lost for good.

They have to get Araf out of the truck. But how?

Hasina and Isak crawl out and run around to the back of the truck.

The truck's cargo box has a long roller door, opened with a chain pulley. Luckily the lock is broken and Zaw Gyi, careless as usual, has left this door a little ajar.

"Araf?" Hasina calls through the crack.

Nothing. She looks at Isak. "I am going to go inside to take a look. You keep watch."

He nods his agreement. She pushes the roller door up as far as she can and slides into the gap.

Inside, the truck is very dark and very, very hot. Hasina quickly feels her skin prickle with sweat. Even worse, the truck stinks of stale urine.

"Araf?" Hasina inches forward in the dark until she

sees what looks like a pair of legs. She creeps closer. And then she finds Araf.

But Araf is not alone. Another little boy is passed out beside him in what looks like a metal cage.

Hasina slides back the bolt and swings the metal door open. She shakes her brother. "Wake up, wake up now. Quick, Araf!"

Araf moans, but then flops back onto the floor.

"Come on, Araf." But it is no good, and Zaw Gyi could be back at any minute. Hasina drags Araf to the roller door. "Isak!" she whispers.

Isak appears in the gap.

"Take Araf." She rolls her half-conscious brother through the gap in the door.

Isak catches him. "I've got him. Come out, Hasina. I think I heard something."

Hasina crawls out and follows Isak to a pile of wood planks. They set Araf down. His eyelids flutter open.

Hasina pats his face. "Wake up, Araf—please."

His eyes open. "Hasina?" His voice is groggy, as if he's been drugged. "I don't want to work in a teashop anymore."

Hasina grins with happiness. "Don't worry. You don't have to." Araf sits up. He is dizzy but okay! She looks at Isak. "There's another boy in there."

"Okay, you keep watch this time. I will get him out," Isak whispers.

"Isak, you will not fit under the door."

Isak hesitates and then nods. "Okay, we go together. If I see Zaw Gyi, I will whistle a warning."

"Araf, if we are not back in ten minutes, you go straight home."

"And no trucks."

"I don't like trucks anymore either," Araf replies.

They creep back to the truck. Once more, Hasina slides beneath the roller door. She holds her breath against the stench as she moves quickly to the body of the truck and reaches into the cage. This boy is smaller than Araf—maybe four or five years old. She shakes him by the shoulder. "Wake up, come on. Wake up!"

But the boy will not wake up. She will have to drag him out too. Just then, Hasina hears a long, low whistle. Zaw Gyi is on his way back.

She drags frantically at the boy in the cage. His foot catches on a metal bar and he gives a dull moan. Hasina stops, untangles it, waits in case Zaw Gyi has heard.

Another whistle, this time louder. And then another.

Suddenly a shadow slices into the light in the back of the truck. Hasina freezes. There is a rumbling sound, and plastic bottles of water roll through the gap and along the floor past her feet. One smashes into the cage. The others smash against the back wall, well out of reach. *Make sure they get water.* This is how Zaw Gyi is obeying U Ko Yin's orders. Hasina can't believe how cruel the man is.

Zaw Gyi walks around to the side of the truck. This is her last chance. She tugs desperately at the boy. He is almost free of the cage. She is so close. All she has to do is drag him a few more meters toward the light.

But then the shadow comes back. Zaw Gyi is at the

roller door, pulling it closed, plunging Hasina into total darkness.

Horror engulfs her. She drops the boy and rushes to the roller door. Can she open it from the inside? She tugs and tugs.

The engine starts up. Exhaust drifts into the box, adding choking fumes to the stink. Hasina starts to panic. She has to get out, or she will be driven out of Teknadaung. From her home, the home she has fought so hard to keep. She will be taken to Sittwe, a town she does not know, with Zaw Gyi. And forced to do what?

She bangs at the door. She kicks at it. She heaves at it with her shoulder. The truck rolls forward. She can feel it bumping over the ground.

Faster and faster it moves. Hasina senses the passage of speed beneath her feet. Still she works frantically at the door. It doesn't matter how fast they are going, she must get out. Now.

And then the truck turns, throwing her first to one side and then back toward the cage. It turns again, sharply, throwing her to the other side, and then brakes hard. Hasina shoots to the back of the truck again, the door she desperately tried to open rearing up out of the darkness like a wall. She smashes hard into metal and then everything goes black.

CHAPTER 27

Hasina wakes again only when light hits her face.

The first thing she feels is incredible thirst. Inside the truck, it must be more than sixty degrees Celsius. Her brain screams for water. She remembers the bottles rolling past her feet. With a free arm she reaches for one.

The second feeling is incredible pain. As soon as she moves her head, it throbs. Light is hurting her eyes after so long in the dark. She shuffles into the shadows.

The third is incredible fear. For now, she remembers: the water, the shadow, this is all Zaw Gyi.

Zaw Gyi stands, staring at her, his mouth wide open. "What are you doing here!"

Crowding in beside him is another man. "Keep your voice down. I don't want the neighbors to know about this." The man takes one look at Hasina. "I didn't order a girl."

"Shh. The neighbors," reminds Zaw Gyi.

"All right," mutters the man nervously, "better bring her inside too." Then he disappears to wherever inside is.

Zaw Gyi reaches for Hasina. She tries to kick at him, but the heat and the injury have made her weak. Bright dots sparkle before her eyes and she passes out again.

When she comes to, Hasina is in a brightly lit room smelling of fresh paint. She can see a big yellow ribbon through the glass door and a freshly painted sign with the words *Just Opening*. This must be the Golden Teashop.

Hasina sits up slowly, cradling her sore head in her hands. She blinks. In front of her is the man she saw at the back of the truck. He must be the owner of the Golden Teashop. He stares at Hasina. "Who are you?"

"Hasina," she answers. "They tried to sell my brother to you."

Zaw Gyi comes back in. A little bell jingles as he opens the door. This time he is carrying the little boy, who is still unconscious, his skin rosy pink from the heat of the truck. Zaw Gyi dumps him in the teashop owner's arms.

"I told you I wanted teashop boys," the man scowls. "Instead, you bring me *one* boy and a girl?"

"There is your boy. There's been a misunderstanding. The girl is merely a complication."

"Humph," scowls the owner. "So what are we going to do with her?"

Hasina wonders the same thing.

Zaw Gyi is shaking his head. He stares hard at Hasina.

"Let me go home. I won't say anything. Please."

"It's too late for that," growls Zaw Gyi.

"Please. I promise."

"We have a contract with your brother. A contract is like a promise. You broke that promise. Now you must pay."

"Araf is too young to make contracts. A lawyer told me that."

"Lawyer," he snarls. "What would you know about lawyers." He looms over her. "You are like a crow." Zaw Gyi spits the words. "Always making a noise. Always pushing in where you're not wanted. Why do you do that, Crow? It is true what they say: a crow may live among peacocks, but a crow may never be a peacock."

Hasina awaits her fate as Zaw Gyi and the teashop owner quarrel in low voices. Her head is pounding, her mouth dry. Worst of all, she realizes she has lost. Her father told her they should stay together. He had been right. She falls asleep to the sound of the men arguing.

She is woken a few hours later by the sound of the bell tinkling as the teashop door opens. She blinks her eyes groggily. At the door is an old man in a business shirt and navy blue plaid *longyi*. Behind him is a tall boy with dark curly hair. The boy looks familiar.

"Excuse me," the man asks in the politest of tones. "Is this the Golden Teashop of Sittwe?"

"Yes," the owner snaps, "but we are closed for the moment."

"Oh, I see," says the man. He turns as if to leave, then turns back again. "I'm so sorry, but is this the only Golden Teashop in Sittwe?"

"Yes, it is," snarls the owner.

"But, like he said, we are closed," growls Zaw Gyi.

The well-dressed man smiles. "Well," he says, "if this is the only Golden Teashop in Sittwe, then that young lady must be Hasina. Hello, Hasina. We spoke on the phone."

So this is Hann Linn, the lawyer Rashid talked about. Zaw Gyi and the teashop owner shoot each other a look.

"Are you the owner of this shop?" the lawyer asks Zaw Gyi.

"No."

"Then you must be the owner."

"Who are you to ask?"

"Let me give you my card. I am a lawyer." The man hands a card to the astonished teashop owner. "Outside, my associates are calling the police. We believe that child trafficking is taking place in the area. And you know the Myanmar government is cracking down …"

The teashop owner shoots Zaw Gyi a nervous glance. "No such thing is taking place here."

"Are you sure? My associates are just asking your neighbors now …"

"No. No such thing here."

Just then, the little boy beside Hasina wakes up. He takes one look around and starts to howl. Zaw Gyi rushes from the shop, the bell clanging as he goes, the teashop owner right behind him.

"Hasina?" The lawyer holds out his hand to her. Hasina takes it and gets to her feet. "Hann Linn at your service. Thank you for your call, my dear. I made a few calls of my own. I can't promise much, but I can promise to help you as best I can."

"Thank you."

Then the man turns to Isak. "And thank you, Isak. It takes a brave man to do what you did. To help those who need it most is true strength." He turns again to Hasina. "This young man hid in the cab of the truck, hung on all the way from Teknadaung."

"Thank you," Hasina says again, and beams at Isak.

"I had some help." Isak holds up the hand phone. "But you are welcome." He smiles his crinkly smile.

Then Hasina turns to the little boy, who is crying softly in the corner. "Would you like to come home with us?"

CHAPTER 28

By the time Hasina arrives home, Dadi Asmah's fever has broken. Within a day or two, she is sitting up and talking. Eating too. Although it will take weeks before Dadi Asmah is better, she is certainly on the mend.

Hasina too needs time to recover from her ordeal. She sleeps—for two and a half days.

While she sleeps, her family grows. Hann Linn does his best, but he cannot find the parents of the small boy Zaw Gyi sold to the Golden Teashop. There are so many like him—children separated from their parents and then lost as families walk to the camps in Bangladesh. The boy's name is Ishin, and it seems only natural that he stay on at the house in Third Mile Street.

Isak and Daamini have agreed to join the household. Dadi Asmah sends Araf and Ghadiya to fetch them. For the moment, Isak sleeps in the hallway between the bedrooms. But already, Isak has begun to build a room separate from the house with offcuts liberated from the construction camp with the help of Cat Girl and Lama.

As for U Ko Yin, the kind Arakanese man is able to help here. Somehow, he makes sure that the stallholders at the bazaar know what U Ko Yin is up to. The bazaar leaders have children of their own, and few of them have the stomach for the way their Muslim neighbors have been treated. They wind up U Ko Yin's sales of AID rice, complaining to the police that he is profiteering. He retreats into his teashop. The few customers he has drift away. Eventually U Ko Yin shuts the Lucky 7 teashop and leaves town.

Zaw Gyi too is dealt with by people's justice. His truck is barred from the construction site as the tale of his misdeeds passes from man to woman to man.

Lama and her family, including Cat Girl, stay in their tent, watching the unharvested rice go yellow and then drop, grain by grain, into the water. When the rains come again, three months on, Lama's family come to stay in the old vegetable garden at Third Mile Street, surrounded by green shoots. But that too is only temporary. They will move on, searching for a place to call their own.

As for the household at Third Mile, life is hard, but there is rice, oil, and salt in the cupboards. And they have each other. Hasina loves sitting with Dadi Asmah, Ghadiya, Araf, and now Ishin, sharing a meal. She loves having Isak close by to talk over things. She doesn't feel so lonely anymore, now that he is here. If only Baba and Mama, Aunt Rukiah and Uncle Rashid were here too.

And then, one day, the hand phone rings. Ghadiya

answers, as usual. Her face bursts into a huge smile. "Hasina! It is for you."

Hasina takes the phone.

"Hello?" calls a familiar voice at the other end.

And then alongside that voice, another. "Hasina? My dear, clever girl."

Hasina's heart swells. Here are the voices she knows and loves. Here are the voices she has been dreaming of. She can barely speak. What words are there?

But as her hands shake, Hasina feels something else. She feels as if the Hasina who has had to defend her family at such great cost has been rejoined by Hasina, the girl who loves soccer and geometry and a boy with a crinkly smile. And her heart, bent and broken, is a little closer to whole again.

She takes a deep breath.

"Hello, Baba? Mama? Is it you?"

AUTHOR'S NOTE

I saw **Rakhine State for** the first time from the air. It was 2014 and I was flying from Thandwe in the south to Sittwe, where this story has its climax. The Bay of Bengal was all manner of blue, the rivers running from the mountains were like silver threads, and the land itself, almost empty of roads, was a deep, extravagant green. It was beautiful.

I was on a tour of exploration then. Myanmar had only been open to the world for a few years. Hillary Clinton, the American secretary of state, visited in 2011. Barak Obama, the American president, visited in 2012. Those who had left the country, like me, were finally returning.

I was born in Rangoon eight months after the 1962 military coup that led to fifty years of military rule. Although I left with my parents as a tiny baby, I have always felt a strong connection to the land of my birth. Especially as my grandparents and great-grandmother remained in Burma until I was in my late teens. The opening up of Myanmar was of great significance to me. On the one hand, I was excited to see this forbidden country; on the other, I was frightened by what I might find, or by what might happen to me while I was there.

My fear was based on the experience of my parents and grandparents. My mother fell pregnant with me when she was a masters student and tutor at Rangoon

University. On July 7, 1962, she had terrible morning sickness and so stayed home. She missed the massacre of students at the hand of army troops on July 7 and 8. My parents could hear the gunfire from their house.

As a child growing up in Canada, I learned to look forward to the blue air letter from my grandparents, written on my grandmother's old manual typewriter. The air letter paper was incredibly thin and light and called onionskin. Postage was by weight and every ounce counted. I remember my mother sending back parcels of things my grandparents could not get: bras, golf balls, socks, toffee, and medicines. They badly wanted light bulbs, but my mother knew these wouldn't survive the trip. We never visited Burma ourselves, as my parents had hoped we would. We weren't allowed visas to return.

My grandmother left Burma after my grandfather died, settling ultimately with my uncle in Seattle, USA. When my grandmother finally came to Canada—and I got to meet her for the first time—she brought few possessions and was in need of supplies. I remember we took her to a shopping mall so she could buy makeup. I was about Hasina's age then. All of a sudden my grandmother stopped dead in the mall, her face pale. "I've forgotten my ID card," she told my mother in a panicked voice. "Don't worry, Mum," my own mother reassured her, "we don't have those here."

I saw the consequences of Myanmar's sad history. Once a kingdom ruled by the Konbaung dynasty, "Burma" was colonized in 1886 by the British, who promptly exiled the royal family and ruled the country as a province of India. During the colonial period, all non-British in Burma were treated as second-class citizens. Burma was granted independence after the Second World War. The new country was immediately plunged into civil war. By the early 1960s, the military decided to step in to keep control.

Military rule was a disaster for the ordinary people of Myanmar. It was the reason my parents chose to leave. The country changed. What was once prosperous became poor. The government, in fear of farther student protests, dismantled the education system. Books, art, the news, and movies were all heavily censored. Parents stopped their children from reading books, because they were frightened reading about new ideas would get their children into trouble. Phones and especially mobile phones were priced so high that ordinary people could not afford them. Owning a mobile phone was equivalent to owning a luxury car. Over those fifty years, Myanmar became what is known as a pariah state—an outcast cut off from the rest of the world.

Fifty years is a long time to be afraid. Which is why it was so exciting for me to visit Myanmar in the early part of this decade—things looked like they were changing. It seemed for the better.

Sadly, while some people in the country have enjoyed greater freedoms, others have not. Their experience of political change has been one of violence and terror and loss. The Rohingya have been victims of this violence in Myanmar. There are others including the Chin and the Kachin.

Flying across the state, it is easy to see one of the reasons why things are so tough in Rakhine. It is a poverty-stricken state. While the green swaths directly beneath my flight path were incredibly beautiful, they also showed that there were hardly any factories or businesses, and with no roads, it would be hard to get crops and fish to market. There is no economic buffer, no safety net. I'd like to say things are changing, but as I write this, there are reports of Arakan Army activity in the state. It would seem the people of Rakhine will have to wait for peace.

TIME LINE

1429 The Kingdom of Mrauk-U, the historical kingdom of Arakan, rules over what is now known as Rakhine State and the Chittagong Division of Bangladesh.

1785-1826 Burmese forces occupy the Arakanese kingdom. The Muslim community in Rakhine expands rapidly during this time. Arakan is ceded to the British after the first Anglo-Burmese War.

1886 After three Anglo-Burmese wars, the predominantly Buddhist Burma becomes the Province of Burma of British India. Arakan is part of this province.

1937 Britain separates Burma Province from British India, making it a crown colony.

Dr. Ba Maw is the first prime minister of Burma until U Saw takes over in 1940.

1942 Japan invades and occupies Burma.

1945 Britain liberates Burma with the help of the Anti-Fascist People's Freedom League led by Aung San.

1947 Aung San and six members of his interim government are assassinated. Local mujahideen in Arakan unite against the government, seeking annexation with Pakistan.

1948 Burma becomes an independent republic with Sao Shwe Thaik as its first president and U Nu as prime minister. Rakhine is part of the independent state of Burma.

1950s Muslim leaders and students in North Arakan use the term *Rohingya* for the region's minority Muslim community.

1960 U Nu's party wins elections, declaring Buddhism the state religion.

1962 A military coup ousts U Nu, establishing a single-party socialist government under General Ne Win. Rohingya rights are farther eroded.

1964 Foreigners are expelled from Burma and independent newspapers banned.

1973 Arakan becomes a state of the Socialist Republic of the Union of Burma, designated as the homeland of the Rakhine people.

1978-91 Government campaigns against the Rohingya push more than 200,000 Muslims into Bangladesh.

1982 The Burmese government's new citizenship law identifies 135 national ethnic groups, excluding the Rohingya, rendering them stateless.

1988 Thousands of Buddhists and Muslims are killed in anti-government riots. The State Law and Order Restoration Council (SLORC) is formed.

Aung San Suu Kyi co-founds and leads the National League for Democracy (NLD).

General Saw Maung seizes power in a military coup. SLORC declares martial law. Burma is renamed Myanmar with Yangon as the new capital. North Arakan is officially known as Rakhine State.

1989 Aung San Suu Kyi is put under house arrest.

1990 The NLD wins the general elections but SLORC refuses to hand over power.

1991 Aung San Suu Kyi is awarded the Nobel Peace Prize.

1992 General Than Shwe is now head of state.

1995 Aung San Suu Kyi is released from house arrest.

2000 Aung San Suu Kyi is again placed under house arrest.

2007 Monks lead almost 100,000 Buddhists in anti-government demonstrations.

2008 Cyclone Nargis strikes. 138,000 people are killed and almost one million are left homeless.

2009 The Arakan Army (AA) is formed to safeguard the Arakanese.

2010 Aung San Suu Kyi is released. The first elections in 20 years are held. The Union Solidarity and Development Party claims victory.

2011 The first parliament in decades is convened in the modern capital, Naypyidaw. Prime Minister Thein Sein is elected president.

2012 Aung San Suu Kyi wins a seat in parliament in Myanmar's first multi-party elections since 1990.

Unrest breaks out in western Rakhine following the alleged rape and murder of a Rakhine Buddhist woman by three Muslims. Escalating communal violence leaves more than 200 dead and close to 150,000 homeless, predominantly Rohingya Muslims.

2013 March Aung San Suu Kyi wins re-election as leader of the NLD.

Deadly clashes between Muslims and Buddhists result in almost 100,000 people being internally displaced, the majority fleeing to Bangladesh by boat.

2014 April The United Nations (UN) Special Rapporteur on Myanmar urges action against possible "crimes against humanity."

2015 The NLD party wins a historic majority. Aung San Suu Kyi becomes state counselor and Htin Kyaw, president.

Approximately 21,000 Rohingya flee to Bangladesh. 8,000 Rohingya are stranded at sea.

2016 About 125,000 people, mainly Rohingya, have been displaced since 2012.

A border post attack in Rakhine State believed to be by Muslim insurgents kills nine police officers. The Myanmar military forcibly removes thousands of villagers from their homes. The situation in Rakhine reaches its lowest point.

The UN and foreign media are blocked from entering northern Rakhine.

2017 February A UN report alleges Myanmar's security forces are waging a brutal campaign of murder, rape, and torture in Rakhine State.

August Myanmar's state media reports the killing of 12 security officers in Rakhine State. The Arakan Rohingya Salvation Army (ARSA) claims responsibility.

September The UN High Commissioner for Human Rights, Zeid Ra'ad Al Hussein, describes the Myanmar military operation as an example of ethnic cleansing.

Aung San Suu Kyi doesn't denounce the alleged atrocities against the Rohingya community.

October According to the International Organization for Migration, 607,000 Rohingya have fled to Bangladesh, 140,000 Rohingya are internally displaced, and 200 villages are left abandoned.

December Médecins Sans Frontières releases a report detailing the death of about 6,700 Rohingya due to the violence in Rakhine State in August and September of 2017.

2018 Aung San Suu Kyi has several international awards and accolades revoked.

Amnesty International reports ARSA allegedly massacred dozens of men, women, and children in Hindu villages in Rakhine State during August 2017.

Violence between AA and security forces escalates in Rakhine State. AA continues to fight for greater independence for ethnic Rakhine Buddhists. Intercommunal violence mounts in northern Shan, Kachin, and other conflict-affected areas in Myanmar.

The UN Security Council envoy visits Myanmar urging a proper investigation into alleged atrocities against the Rohingya in Rakhine State.

GLOSSARY

BENGALI

daamini   lightning

BURMESE

boothi   vegetable like zucchini

chaung   small stream

chinlone   woven rattan ball

htamein   wraparound skirt for females

jaggery   palm sugar in blocks, eaten after meals or as a sweet

kalama   insult used against Indian women meaning "foreigner"

kyat   Myanmar currency

longyi   long wraparound skirt worn by men and women

mingalar bar   Myanmar greeting

nagar   dragon; mythical creature in Myanmar fairytales

Pathein   region of Myanmar and type of rice

saya   respectful term for teacher

sein pan   golden mohur tree with bright orange flowers

shi-kho   polite greeting

stupa	place of meditation
taing-yin-thar	"native" of Burma prior to colonization—a contested term
thakin	sir
thanaka	sweet-smelling powder used as sunscreen; tree bark used in traditional makeup

MRO LANGUAGE

hom, tui	paddy field
Mro-*cha*	person of the Mro ethnic group

ROHINGYA

aasso-lamu alaikum	has Allah kept you well?
Asr	afternoon prayer
azan	call to prayer
baba	father, daddy
babi	sister-in-law
bazu	cotton top
bismillah karo hamam rahin	in the name of Allah, gracious and merciful
dadi	grandmother
deshi	cooking pot
Dhurh	general term for prayer; also the term used for second prayers of the day just before lunch
dut	condensed milk

Eid al-Adha	festival of the sacrifice
Fagr	first morning prayer
hodu hak	fried calabash; a long gourd
hori hak	pumpkin leaf with garlic
ken ah so?	how are you?
madrassa	schoolroom
Maghirb	dusk prayer
maja-fu	father's sister
mama	mother
massor salon	fish curry
mohzeem	one who calls to prayer
numal	veil (headscarf) that Muslim women wear in public
shamish	spoon
suri	knife
tufih	cap
wa alaikum aasso-lam	yes, Allah has kept me well

SHAN LANGUAGE

lawl ait	special bag known locally as a "Shan bag"

URDU

kameez	Indian top
tiffin	lunch

ACKNOWLEDGMENTS

Thanks to my parents, Pam and Jim, for their personal insights into the country that was Burma and is now Myanmar. Their stories made me a writer. To Warren and Julian, who raised pertinent questions throughout the writing process. To Peter and Nancy, who provided a conducive space for rewrites. To Sierra, who lent me her cat, Winston, and allowed me to transplant him from icy Quebec to tropical Rakhine and rename him (now her) Daamini. Thanks also to my early reader, Mattie.

Writing a book about dramatic and sensitive events requires solid research. I have tried to make this story as accurate as possible. I am indebted to Dr. Anthony Ware for sharing his research and recommend his book *Myanmar's 'Rohingya' Conflict*, co-authored by Costas Laoutides, published by Hurst in 2018.

I would also like to thank the members of Melbourne's Rohingya community who helped with cultural and linguistic details. In particular, Tara Begum, who graciously opened her home to me, fed me *dosa* and introduced me to her family. Thanks also to Shakilah Ibrahim who read the book and offered feedback on cultural details. Tara Begum and Shakilah Ibrahim translated most of the Rohingya words in the text and offered phonetic spellings. I am also grateful to Nurankis Ibrahim who did such a great job posing for the original cover of the Australian edition. Wajidah patiently answered my many questions and showed me her call-to-prayer clock, which was the inspiration for Ibrahim's gift to Nurzamal. Habib Ibrahim introduced me to his community in a Springvale restaurant that sells Rohingya foods including Nurzamal's favorite spice blend.

The character of the Sittwe lawyer is loosely based on the 2018 winner of the Aurora Prize for Awakening Humanity, Kyaw Hla Aung.

May Kyel Winn translated the Burmese words in this text and helped me with details of Myanmar culture and politics. The Australia Myanmar Institute runs events that give up-to-the minute insights into contemporary Myanmar. It was at one lecture that I realized the book needed to open with the helicopters and at another when I understood the significance of smartphones and social media to Myanmar politics.

Thanks to the writers and researchers in the non/fictionLab, NoveLab, as well as my neighbors in the Writer's Wing at the Abbotsford Convent for their fellowship and conversations around what a novel can and cannot do.

A big thanks to Lyn White and the publishing and editorial staff at Allen & Unwin, including Sophie Splatt, copy editor Hilary Reynolds, and proofreader Sonja Heijn who whipped the book into shape.

This book was made possible through the support of Creative Victoria and the Australia Council. In 2014, I spent ten weeks in Myanmar as an Asialink Resident, funded by Creative Victoria, and as a guest of the New Zero Gallery, Yangon.

FIND OUT MORE ABOUT...

Myanmar

https://www.britannica.com/place/Myanmar

https://www.youtube.com
    Search for "Geography Now! MYANMAR"

The Rohingya

https://www.news.com.au
    Search for "Who are the Rohingya and what is happening in Myanmar?"

https://www.abc.net.au/news
    Search for "Stateless Rohingya pushed from Myanmar, but unwanted by Bangladesh"

https://www.aljazeera.com
    Search for "Who are the Rohingya?"

The Rohingya crisis

https://www.bbc.com
    Search for "Myanmar Rohingya: What you need to know about the crisis"

https://www.youtube.com
    Search for "The Rohingya crisis in 90 seconds"

The following clip contains images that some viewers may find distressing:
https://www.youtube.com
    Search for "Rohingya crisis: the world's fastest growing humanitarian crisis—BBC News"